"What a comfort you are to a man, Miranda," said Mr. Glendower.

On those words his voice dropped to a gentleness which was almost caressing, and she flushed and could not meet his gaze.

"Modest Miranda. Can this be the storm maiden who returned my kiss with fire?"

"I was not . . . not myself. I do not think it honorable of you to refer to it. I behaved with great impropriety."

Mr. Glendower laughed, but it was a bitter sound. "Come here, Miranda."

Unwillingly she walked to him and stood motionless, staring at her feet. He put a finger under her chin and tilted her face, forcing her to look into his eyes. Their message was unmistakable. She knew she should pull herself away, but she was mesmerized. "I love you, Miranda. But your honor will not admit of any such passion, will it? Beautiful, adorable Miranda. I love you and I think you care for me."

"Oh, why did you speak?" She tore herself away from him, and her voice was a wail of anguish. "Now I cannot stay here."

"You will not go." He grasped her wrist and held it cruelly tight. "You shall not leave me. You shall not, I say. I will not let you."

Autumn Lace

Eileen Jackson

A FAWCETT CREST BOOK

Fawcett Publications, Inc., Greenwich, Connecticut

AUTUMN LACE

THIS BOOK CONTAINS THE COMPLETE TEXT OF
THE ORIGINAL HARDCOVER EDITION.

A Fawcett Crest Book reprinted by arrangement with
Walker Publishing Company, Inc.

ISBN: 0-449-23297-2

Featured Selection of the Young Adult's Division of the
Literary Guild, November 1976

Printed in the United States of America

10 9 8 7 6 5 4 3 2 1

Autumn Lace

Chapter One

Paddington Station was an echoing cavern filled with hurrying men and noise from the engines emitting smoke and steam. With Papa's haversack slung over her slender shoulder, clutching her battered portmanteau and Mama's tapestry Dorothy bag, which contained all her money, bread, cheese and apples and a book for the journey, Miranda Courtney found her way to a first-class compartment on the Barmouth train.

It was empty, but for safety's sake she deposited her book in one corner, her portmanteau in another and herself in a third, then she leaned back and closed her eyes for a moment of calm. It was still only a quarter to ten, so presumably Mrs. Mowbray and her daughter would not arrive for at least ten minutes.

A mixture of excitement, nervousness and worry had wearied her, and she began to float in a haze of sleep in which she suddenly heard Mama's voice calling her urgently. But dear Mama would never have sounded so harsh, and she certainly would not have addressed her as Matilda.

"Matilda Courtney! How dare you sleep when you should be looking out for us. Oblige me by moving your belongings, and Miss Ellen and I will be seated."

Mrs. Mowbray, in a tweed travelling costume, was standing over her. "Thank you, porter, you may place the hamper beneath my seat. Be seated, Ellen. Here is your ticket, Matilda. I am sure you will have no difficulty in finding your way to your carriage."

Still dazed, Miranda gathered her possessions and left. The porter gave her a friendly grin. "Now then, missy, you've got into mischief, haven't you? Fancy falling asleep like that. Come on, I'll show you where you should be."

As Miranda discovered that for the first time in her twenty-one years she was not to travel first class, she felt a moment's wild rebellion. However short of money dear Papa had been, he had insisted on the genteel way of transport for his women-folk for even the shortest journey. Then her shoulders sagged as she comprehended the futility of minding, and she entered the door pointed out by the porter.

Staring out of the window as the train began its journey, she scarcely saw the landscape as her mind roamed over the events of the past days. Walter would have been very angry when he discovered her note telling him of her plans. In fact, now that she had time to think, she began to question her wisdom. Swaying on the wooden bench, listening to the monotonous clickety-clack of the wheels, it seemed she must be in some bad dream from which she would awake to find herself back in the parsonage, which had been her life-long home with dear Mama and Papa.

But those days were gone never to return, and she had felt grateful to her brother, Walter, for his offer of a home when their parents died within days of each other in the influenza epidemic in the Autumn of 1877. Was it only a year ago when, sick with grief at her loss, she had been received into her brother's home? Her gratitude for the sanctuary had been swiftly eroded by the insatiable demands made upon her by Walter's wife, who clearly regarded her as an unpaid servant to her brood of unruly children.

Even so, necessity and family duty might have carried her on, but the discovery of Walter's plans had been the final unbearable burden.

The scene in the study was still hideously clear in her mind when she had cried out, "Walter, you would not have me marry a man I do not care for. Worse, he is repellent to me."

"Nonsense! What does such a young girl as you know of these matters? As I have explained, Miranda, this alliance would amalgamate my bookshop with James's, and I must tell you that I need a larger income. My dear wife is once more expecting a happy event, and you can best show your appreciation of all we have done for your by obeying me in this. And James is a most presentable young man:"

"Young!"

"He is no more than five and forty. That is no age for a man—in fact it is a most suitable age for marriage—for a man that is—and you will never receive a better offer. Your handsome appearance has made you arrogant, but beauty doesn't last forever, and you discourage any man who looks twice at you. What is it you want of a husband?"

"I don't know. I only know that I have met no one I could tolerate in the ... the intimacy of marriage."

"Miranda! This is indelicate talk! And what is wrong with James?"

Almost speechless in her inability to impress her brother with her disgust at the proposed alliance, Miranda said the first thing she thought of. "He ... he has clammy hands."

"Guard your tongue, miss." Walter's moustaches quivered in a way which would have made her giggle had the situation been less serious. "How could Papa have allowed you to develop in so frivolous a manner?"

"He and Mama would not have tried to force me into a distasteful marriage."

"Then if you do not marry James, what will you do? Spend your life here? Of course, your sister-in-law finds you useful and will do so increasingly as the years pass, though I cannot answer for harmony between you when she discovers that a most beneficial business alliance between James and myself has been destroyed by your wilful behaviour."

Miranda shuddered. "I can find work. This is the nineteenth century, not the dark ages."

"And pray what can *you* do?"

"I can sew!" Miranda forgot herself sufficiently almost to yell.

Walter emitted an explosive sound. "I will send James to you when he arrives tomorrow. Beggars cannot be choosers, my girl."

Miranda held her head proudly. "I am not quite a beggar, Walter."

"You have a miserable forty pounds. Papa was a fool. Oh, I'm sorry to have to say so, but if he had not given his substance to every beggar in the parish, you might have had a dowry. Instead, you must take the best offer you get, and I'll hear no more talk of likes and dislikes."

Between them they would have worn down her resistance, Miranda knew, and that was why she had crept out of her brother's house and begun the journey which had led her to stumble into Mrs. Gash's London Servant's Home and Registry just as it was closing for the night.

Her awakening in the following dawn had brought home to her what a difficult path she had chosen. Her sensitive nose had wrinkled at the mingled odours and heavy breathing of strange women, and before she was properly awake the door to the attic dormitory was thrown open with the abruptness of a pistol shot and the grim-faced Mrs. Gash called, "Rise at once! Make your ablutions, tidy your beds and sweep the floor. Breakfast will be in half an hour from now at seven. Anyone who is late or appears in a state of undress will be excluded from the meal."

Miranda was quick to leap up and pad to the nearest wash bowl, where she sluiced her face and hands, deploring the lack of privacy which prevented her usual sponge-bath, and when she saw that the dilatory risers had to use the same water she felt glad she had been prompt.

She dressed in some embarrassment beneath the watchful gaze of a girl in the next bed, adjusting the lace at the throat and wrists of her blue foulard dress and brushing her brown curls into glossiness before tying them back with a matching blue ribbon.

The girl chuckled. "It's plain to see you ain't been in service before."

Miranda's deep-blue eyes stared at her.

"Just let old Ma Gash get a gander at your fol-der-rols and your hair like that, and she'll scream fit to bust her stays."

"But . . . but should I not appear at my best?"

"This is a servant's registry, not a marriage market,

and let any of the female diamond squad see you like that, and they won't give you the time o' day. It's their husbands and sons, see. Seems you can't trust a gentry cove with a pretty wench. How old are you?"

"Twenty-one, but I have not sought employment before, and I *am* inexperienced." Miranda touched her curls nervously. "Please—could you tell me how I should go on?"

"Righto, ducks. Name's Bet. I'm what's called a general —all muscles and no airs and graces like a work horse. Wouldn't be here, but I thought I'd try me luck on a farm. Ha! You can stow yer country life. Give me the town. So I'm out of a place, but not for long."

While she talked, she untied the blue ribbon and brushed Miranda's hair vigorously. "I'll soon find me a mistress. I always get sent to places where they can't afford more'n one servant, and there's plenty like that."

She twisted Miranda's hair into a wincingly tight knot, which she secured with large, ugly hairpins from her pocket.

"Now, if you've got scissors, take the lace from your dress. Here, give them to me, your hands are shaking."

She snipped at the delicate stitches. "It's a crying shame that such as you should be brought to a place like this. You've got to be tough to live."

She gestured with her thumb down the room. "There's old Miss Lacy again. It's my belief Ma Gash only keeps her here for the seven and a tanner she gets from her for her board. When her money's gone, she'll be out. Started as a governess, but her wind's broken."

Miranda stared with horror at the exhausted face and emaciated body of the elderly woman. "What will become of her?"

Bet shrugged. "Who knows? She might be lucky and get into a home for retired gentlewomen, but I think you need a bit o' blunt for that, and hers must be near gone or she'd not be here at her age. She'll most likely end up starving on the Embankment with the others.

"There, that's the lace gone. Now listen, girl, when you meet a likely mistress, try to look stern, and for pity's sake keep your twinklers down. You must look

11

humble, see, however you feel. And watch yerself, ducky, 'cos there's folk in London who'll pretend to help you and land you in a life of dirt you'll not escape from. Understand?"

Miranda gathered enough of what Bet was saying to know that she talked good sense, and she nodded. "Thank you, Bet. It's good of you to bother."

"You two goin' to be all day!" yelled a woman at the end of the room. "We'm doin' all the work while you blab."

"Aw, keep yer red rag in yer pimple," shrieked Bet, then ignoring the woman's reply said to Miranda, "What sort o' work you lookin' for?"

"I thought perhaps a seamstress. There are places for sewing women I think . . ."

"Oh, my Gawd, it's a good thing Bet was here today. D'you fancy yerself as a shirt maker? Two dozen a day at sevenpence the dozen. Or a buttonholer at a halfpence each? You're like a lamb to the slaughter. If you must work, then find yerself a private house. Promise 'em anything, but get yerself a comfy place. How good is your sewing?"

"I made the lace on my dress—and the dress, of course."

"Did you, though." Bet fingered the lace with coarse hands, which were unexpectedly reverent. "Well, I wish you luck."

Miranda picked up the froth of lace and held it out. "Bet, I'm so grateful to you. Would you, perhaps, do me the honour of accepting this as a gift. It . . . it's little enough."

Bet's rosy face became redder with pleasure. "Do you the honour! I should say so. Won't my cove think I'm fine when he sees this."

After a breakfast of coarse oatmeal and weak tea, Miranda stood in Mrs. Gash's office, where she was questioned. "Not a single reference? How do you expect me to place you? You might be anybody."

"I . . . I can give the names of respectable people who will vouch for me," ventured Miranda.

Mrs. Gash studied the names and addresses Miranda wrote out for her. "H'm, a doctor, a parson and a Justice of the Peace. Well, you wouldn't dare presume on them without a right. They'd soon set the law on you, if you did. And you say you're of age so no one can fetch you back. You look respectable, and it's clear you've been gently reared. I dare say it'll do. Why are you here?"

She shot the question so abruptly that Miranda blurted out the truth. "I ran away from an unwelcome suitor. My . . . my brother would not support me in my refusal."

"Hoity toity! I wouldn't have thought you could afford to be so choosy. Well, there's no accounting for some women."

She scribbled on the sheet of paper, then her face cracked into a grimace. "Dame Fortune may have smiled on you, Miranda Courtney, though your headstrong flight from your brother's protection does not entitle you to luck. I have a Mrs. Augusta Mowbray arriving soon. She is looking for a resident seamstress and asks particularly that a girl of good character be found as she will be asked to instruct two young ladies in the art of needlework. So far, I have been unable to satisfy her. Mrs. Mowbray is to take charge of her cousin's house as his wife's health is failing. You will not mind travelling to Wales!"

"N . . . no, of course not."

Miranda was beginning to understand why Mrs. Gash ran a successful servant's registry. The terrifying staccato delivery of her questions must have startled many a poor young girl into taking an unwanted post. But if she removed into Wales, she would be more inaccessible, and Walter hated going to a lot of trouble.

Bet found a place first. "My new missus has got a face like a hatchet, but times are hard. I told her I'd be along later today. I want to see if you have any luck."

Before Miranda could reply to this heart-warming concern, she was sent for to go to the interview room. She knocked on the door, though the hammering of her heart must surely have given warning of her approach.

The room was sparsely furnished, and seated in the best chair was the woman who might hold her future. Dressed from head to toe in black, Mrs. Mowbray stared hard at Miranda, then slowly turned her head. "Mrs. Gash, you informed me that this person was unused to domestic service, but it will be impossible for me to employ a girl who has not the remotest idea of how to behave towards her betters."

As Mrs. Gash tutted and murmured, Mrs. Mowbray continued to Miranda, "You say you are a parson's daughter. Did your Papa employ servants?"

Miranda remembered the two sturdy village girls who were as much friends as domestic servants, and answered, "Yes."

"Then you should know it is your place always to curtsey to your employer. Mrs. Gash, I do not know that this young woman will suit. I had not reckoned on having to begin training her."

"She is intelligent, madam, she will learn quickly, I'm sure."

Miranda thought, they talk of me as if I were not here. Was this to be the pattern of her future life? She looked at the slightly built young woman who sat near Mrs. Mowbray. She wore an ugly gown of tan French poplin and a brown shawl. Her hair was of silvery gold of the thin silkiness which was so difficult to dress to advantage, and even now her cream straw hat with its tan ribbons was sliding to one side. She stared at Miranda with eyes of pale blue in a pallid face, then sighed as if she was bored.

"Miss Courtney!" Mrs. Gash's voice was sharp with fury. This stupid girl had seemed to offer possibilities, but now it appeared she was without any native sense at all and a dreamer, too.

Miranda started. "I beg your pardon, Mrs. Gash. I had not known you were addressing me."

She remembered Miss Lacy and realised that this chance of a position was sliding from her. She needed it urgently, and she looked at Mrs. Mowbray, saying as humbly as she could, "I beg your pardon also, ma'am, but I was taken with the appearance of the young lady. I regret my apparent absence of manners."

Mrs. Mowbray raised a lorgnette, and Miranda, remembering Bet's strictures, modestly lowered her eyes. "Mrs. Gash," pronounced the pacified lady, "this person may suit me after all." She patted the unresponsive hand of her companion. "This is my daughter, Miss Ellen, for whom you will also be sewing, and she is one of the young ladies whom it will be your duty to instruct. Miss Ellen fancies she does not care to sew, but I think she must change her mind. The other pupil is the daughter of my cousins, Mr. and Mrs. Glendower of Ynys Noddfa, Merionethshire. They are your employers and have entrusted to me the choice of a seamstress."

"Have they no seamstresses in Wales?" asked Miranda.

There was a pregnant silence before Mrs. Mowbray again raised her lorgnette, and Miranda flushed. "I should not have spoken so precipitately."

"No, you should not. Yes, I suppose there must be sewing women in Wales, and, in fact, I think one is employed for plain sewing, but Mr. Glendower requires one who can do more than merely sew for the ladies. Both his wife and his daughter require instructive amusement. And before we proceed to a definitive engagement and to terms, I must see a sample of your work."

"I made my gown and—" instinctively, Miranda's hand went to her throat—"the lace on my . . ." Then she stopped, remembering her gift to Bet, ". . . . on my . . . drawers," she finished in embarrassed tones.

"You can make lace? Bobbin or needlepoint?"

"Both," answered Miranda, "but I prefer needlepoint. Papa had an Italian parishioner who taught me the art."

"A rare accomplishment indeed these days," asserted Mrs. Mowbray before she remembered her purpose. "H'm, well, a girl who hires herself out to sew should be familiar with all its branches. Shew me the lace."

Miranda's delicate skin flushed as she hesitated, and Mrs. Gash exclaimed, "No need for such false modesty. We are all females here."

Miranda raised her skirts until the legs of her drawers were visible and drew closer to Mrs. Mowbray when she beckoned.

"Passable," murmured that lady as she fingered the exquisite stitchery. "Of course, you would not expect high wages in view of your inexperience. I can offer you eighteen pounds a year and not a penny more."

Miranda had no idea of bargaining and even less of whether or not she was being cheated, so she said simply, "Thank you very much."

15

Mrs. Mowbray rose. "Thank you, Mrs. Gash. Come, Ellen, we must purchase materials before we leave. We will see if Swan and Edgar still have the lengths of cashmere and mohair."

She strode to the door followed by the languid Ellen, then turned. "Oh, by the way, Miranda, you will be ready to leave Paddington Station for Barmouth on the ten o'clock train tomorrow morning. Please be clothed in a discreet manner suited to your position. And I should advise you to purchase velveteen, for the Welsh coastal winter can be severe, and velveteen is quite like velvet and will do well enough for you.

"I shall purchase your railway ticket—Mr. Glendower has supplied me with funds—and your initial duty will be to procure seats for Miss Ellen and myself in a first-class compartment.

"You must also provide your own food for the journey as the stops do not allow much time for taking refreshment."

She swept out without looking back, giving Miranda a propitious opportunity to quell the rebellious feelings which almost threatened to choke her.

"Eighteen pounds a year!" Bet exploded, "that's no more than a good housemaid can ask these days. This Glendower man must be a regular old flint."

"I didn't know," said Miranda, "should I have asked more?"

Bet gave a gusty sigh. "I reckon not, ducks, but you'll learn. I hope you don't get too bruised, that's all." She picked up her bundle. "I'm off then. Good luck to you, gel."

Miranda watched her departure feeling as if she was losing her only friend. She jumped as Mrs. Gash appeared. "So you'll be here one more night. You realise, of course, that a percentage of your wages will come to me from Mrs. Mowbray, who'll stop it from you." At Miranda's astonished look she scoffed, "Well, you don't expect to eat for nothing, do you? How d'you think I live?"

"I imagined that prospective employers . . ."

"Then you thought wrong. Oh, and another thing, Mrs.

Mowbray says your name won't do at all, and I agree with her. From now on you're to be Matilda."

Miranda set her lips tight. To have answered would have released the tears. In the afternoon she took an omnibus to Oxford Street and visited Peter Robinson's Store, where she bought serge in suitably drab shades and some lengths of velveteen to make jackets.

She wandered about for a while, revelling in the displays of rich materials until her eyes were caught by some shimmering brocade of the blue-green colour of the sea she had once seen beneath a darkening sky. In an instant she was back with Mama and Papa in a world of content where there was time to watch the glories of nature and almost without volition found herself ordering a piece of the material. At twelve and sixpence a yard she could afford only a little, so purchased some silver-grey ribbed silk to complete the dress she had in mind. It was only as she left the store that it dawned on her that she would have no opportunity for wearing such a garment.

A baby's cry plucked her from the past to the present discomfort of swaying on the train's wooden bench where it was impossible either to doze or to compose her mind to her book, and the five-hour journey to Chester seemed interminable. She wondered if she would ever develop the composure of the young mother who suckled her child placidly beneath her coarse shawl.

At Chester she was glad to stretch her legs, but her cheaper mode of travel did not permit her to enter the rooms reserved for ladies of quality. Another pin-prick of irritation. She began to realise that Walter had spoken with some truth when he had ridiculed the idea of her earning a living, but the thought of returning was unendurable. I'll not be beaten, she vowed, somewhere I'll make a place for myself.

The stop scarcely allowed time for buying food, and Miranda munched at her own fare thankfully as the train sped on. Then it crossed the border into Wales, and she watched the scenery with increasing delight as they huffed their way between lush grazing fields and through rock cuttings, which opened on to panoramas of heart-catching beauty.

As the train began to make frequent stops at small stations, it occurred to Miranda that she was in a land which spoke a different language, and she felt even more isolated. Was she to be among people to whom she could never talk?

At exactly seven o'clock they pulled into Barmouth Junction, where she joined Mrs. Mowbray and Miss Ellen, still neat in her brown and beige suit and hat, which were as hideously unbecoming as her garb of yesterday. Miranda supposed her mother chose her clothes as she seemed to lack any enterprise.

Mrs. Mowbray paused in her loud instructions regarding her mountain of luggage. "Ah, there you are, Matilda, please accompany Miss Ellen to the train, which awaits us. I must direct these men. How slow they are. I daresay the five-minute bell has already rung. How provoking that one cannot speak to the porters in a language they can understand."

A young porter touched his cap. "Some of us have learned the English, ma'am. We need it, you see, such a lot of people coming to visit our beautiful Barmouth."

Mrs. Mowbray was not put out. "Then why did not you say so before? Handle my goods with care. I have had to pay a considerable sum in excess baggage. The charges are disgraceful."

Miranda helped Ellen into a first-class carriage and was surprised when Mrs. Mowbray ordered her to join them for the remainder of the journey, but she forgot her discomforts of the past hours as the train began to puff slowly across a bridge thrown over a wide expanse of water. "Oh, how lovely," she cried, forgetting her new lack of status, "what is it called?"

Mrs. Mowbray snorted, but to Miranda's surprise, Ellen said, "It is the Mawddaoh Estuary, and this the longest bridge in Wales. It is a great feat of engineering."

Her voice was as colourless as her appearance, but Miranda caught a glint in her pale eyes which could have been of pleasure or excitement. She wondered if Ellen would have developed a personality had she not been so obviously dominated by her mother.

She continued to gaze at the beauty around them, and

thought she must find content here. How could she fail to do so? But within the hour her spirits had swung back to dejection as they alighted at the little station of Aber-lliw.

A man strode towards them and briefly kissed Mrs. Mowbray and Ellen. "Welcome, cousins, I trust you had a good journey."

"It was far too long, Cousin Gethin," complained Mrs. Mowbray, but she had lost his attention as his gaze went past her to Miranda, who stared back at him.

So this was Gethin Glendower of the tight purse. He was a little under six feet and powerfully built. He could have been mistaken for a bailiff, she thought, in tweeds which were well cut, but worn, and highly polished boots, which had seen much service. Evidently his cheese-paring ways extended to himself as well as to his dependents. He was clean shaven, and two deep furrows were scored from his nostrils to the corners of his shapely mouth. Faint lines on his brow betrayed his tendency to frown. He looked to be about thirty-seven or -eight, and he had not once smiled. Her courage sank lower. What kind of life would be hers between the rudely autocratic Mrs. Mowbray, Ellen who seemed without spirit or charm, this bad-tempered-looking man and servants who talked a language foreign to her?

Mr. Glendower spoke. "I hope you are not a star-gazer. We have no need of any useless females here."

His voice was well modulated, but cool, and Miranda forgot herself. "I can do any work required of me," she flashed, "and I'll save my dreaming for my own time—that is, if I am granted any."

The man's brows lifted. "You are not what I expected. Where did my cousin kidnap you?"

"I came from choice. I . . . I am the daughter of a gentleman—my . . . my circumstances have dictated that I must earn my living."

Her chin had gone up as she spoke, though inwardly she quaked. This man had the power to move her to timidity, but to her surprise he smiled at her reply, and the harshness in his face was wiped out for an instant before again he looked grim. "You're a regular little fire-eater, but I do assure you we will try to treat you with the respect you feel you deserve. No doubt time will teach you that you do not generally address your employers as if you were their equal in station. For myself, I am accustomed to be called 'sir'. Is that understood?"

Miranda fought down her chagrin and managed to apologise. "I . . . I forgot myself. I am not used to domestic service—sir."

"Thank you. That is better. And now here comes someone to carry your luggage. You see, we do not expect females to struggle with heavy weights, be they ever so humble."

She caught the mockery in his eyes before he turned away, and she followed him, clutching Mama's Dorothy bag as if it were a life-line. She felt she might need one in the months ahead.

Chapter Two

The party emerged into a narrow, hedged lane, heavy with the scents of late summer flowers, and Miranda swallowed incipient tears as she remembered when she and Papa had walked between similar hedges and she had filled her hands with honeysuckle, celandines and hare-bells.

Lost for a moment in her memories, she was surprised to realize that no carriage awaited them. Instead there was a line of small, sturdy ponies, some with the luggage strapped to their backs, and Mrs. Mowbray and Ellen were already mounted.

Mrs. Mowbray said, impatiently, "You can ride, I suppose, Matilda." Her tones dared her to deny it, and Miranda nodded, unwilling to admit before the whole company that her sole experience had been garnered on the backs of huge slow farm horses as a child, or later, riding or driving the stubborn old donkey, which was all her Papa could afford to keep.

She held out her foot, and the broad shouldered servant threw her into the saddle. She had time only to gather the reins before they moved off.

The pony seemed docile, but Miranda was relieved to see the servant go to its head and begin to lead it after the others. The pack horses were strung together in a line, and the two ladies of the party rode similar mounts as her own, but Gethin Glendower was astride a powerful grey, which pranced and sidled across the lane till he had gentled it to obedience with a voice caressing in its tenderness, then he moved to the head of the procession.

Some of the servants wore smart brown and blue

livery and others a good grey cloth and strong boots, while the horses were in prime condition, their harness of first-quality leather and shining brass, yet their employer gave the appearance of a man who found it difficult to make ends meet. But he could have ridden a mule, Miranda decided, and that proudly held head and the arrogance which seemed to emanate even from his back would have proclaimed him master here.

As if sensing her eyes upon him, he turned suddenly to look at her and she jerked her head away.

The hedges were lower now, and scrubby, and Miranda could see over them into open grassland, where a solitary lap-wing ran about, its crested head bobbing in the constant search for food. When she looked again to the front, a bend had brought them to a view which made her gasp. A carpet of green foliage lay before them and beyond it a huge expanse of sand running to the foot of a hill on which was built a large stone dwelling, which seemed to crouch and sprawl across the hillside as if for protection. Beyond, the sea shimmered with points of jewelled sunlight.

The servant heard her gasp and looked up grinning. " 'Tis a bit of a sight when you see it for the first time, isn't it, miss?"

"Yes, indeed. Oh, you speak English! I am so relieved. I thought I was to be quite isolated here. I hadn't realized when I took the post . . ."

"You a servant, then? You don't look like one, nor yet sound like one neither."

"I assure you I am. I am a seamstress. Mrs. Mowbray engaged me in London. But she did not tell me I should be on an . . . an . . . what exactly is that hill, Mr. . . .?"

"Name's Dafydd. You needn't call me mister."

"I'm Mir . . . Matilda."

"How are you, Matilda? Nice to meet you."

He waved a hand towards the front. "The land ahead is a kind of island, see. It's completely cut off when the tide comes up the estuary. I expect you were surprised not to be fetched by a carriage, but you'll understand in a minute."

The leading ponies had begun to trek over flat greenery

ahead, and now Miranda's guide led her after them. She looked down at Dafydd's feet as she heard the squelching and realised that they were walking through marsh grass.

Dafydd smiled kindly. "No need to worry, Matilda, but now you see why we travel this way. These ponies could pick their way across on their own, so well do they know the path, but the master insists that guests and newcomers are always led most careful like. I reckon you'll learn to manage without help if you stay long enough."

Miranda shook a little and clung to the pommel as the ponies' hooves sank and sucked at the soft sand beneath the green. "It's the tide has made it so wet today," explained Dafydd. "Often the water don't reach this far, then it's dry, but we're having our higher tides at present, so it could be dangerous. But as long as we stay on the track we're fine. I've worked here since I was a lad and know the path blind-fold, so don't look so fearful."

"I'm sorry. I am a little nervous of water. A nurse-maid I had was careless and I nearly drowned in a stream . . ." She stopped, realising that to talk of her nurse to a fellow servant could be considered pretentious, but Dafydd grinned. "I knew you wasn't the usual type of girl we get here for a maid. You'd best watch out for Mrs. Pritchett, she's the housekeeper and rules the staff with an iron rod. Mr. Merrick—he's the butler—is softer. Well, he is to pretty wenches. Come to think of it," glancing appreciatively at her, "you'd best have an eye to him as well."

The pink rose to Miranda's face, and she asked hastily, "How is it that you speak English so well? The people who boarded the train used only Welsh."

"It's a rule here when you're taken on in the big house that you learn the English, so you'll be able to make friends, I daresay. You'll need to, I'm thinking, for not many village folk talk your language."

"I saw no village."

"It's the other direction from the station. I was born there and lived there till I came here to the kitchen at ten years old. Then I moved to the stables, where I always wanted to be. I love horses I do."

The cavalcade was now well out on to the sand which was not so flat as it had appeared from a distance, and rose in hillocks to descend into pools in which small fish flipped out of sight. Some of the pools they were able to splash through; others, which they skirted, must often have been several feet in depth.

Gethin Glendower still headed the procession. He did not look round, and Miranda felt an irrational irritation. It was as if he expected everyone to follow precisely where he led. I'm going this way, his back seemed to pronounce, and if you can't follow me so much the worse for you.

Dafydd, who seemed quick to sense her feelings, grinned again. "He's not being unsociable, see, this is the time of the high tides. You'd not know we had a storm last night, would you, 'tis so calm today, but when the sea comes in fast it can shift the sand. Mr. Glendowner is making sure the ladies don't get a bath they wouldn't relish."

Miranda laughed aloud at the idea of Mrs. Mowbray's dignity suddenly quenched in a pool, and was abashed as that haughty lady looked round to give her a frown.

"Naughty girl," said Dafydd, beneath his breath. "In future, Matilda, remember to laugh only in the kitchen."

Miranda suppressed a giggle with difficulty as she asked, "Why doesn't your master build a path across here?"

"I don't know, for sure, but he's a private sort of man. When the tide's full in, you can cross by boat, but not easily. The water swirls round so fast round Ynys Noddfa that the currents gets real powerful. I don't think he wants it made easy for folks to reach him."

"Ynys Noddfa," mused Miranda, "that's the name of Mr. Glendower's residence."

"So 'tis—and the name of the island, too. It's the only dwelling there except for the home farm, and it's been in the family for generations. It means Island of Refuge in your tongue."

Miranda stared hard at the house and shivered a little at the harshly inhospitable looking grey stones, which seemed to belie their name. Now that they were nearer, she could see that the house was built in more than one style. "It looks as if no one could decide what to add next," she exclaimed.

Dafydd gave her his quick smile. "A very long time ago it was a farm house, but as the Glendowers got richer, each owner built more. Mostly they tried to match what went before, but the present lady don't care for old places, and that's why the bit on the end is the way it is."

As Miranda jogged along she wondered what sort of a woman would authorise so unattractive a structure. The latest wing rose some way above the rest and was adorned with crenellations and a turret and gave incongruity to the house. "Modern Gothic," she murmured, "my papa never cared for it." Dafydd gave her a quick glance as if feeling her sadness, but said nothing as they climbed the grassy hill and entered iron gates, which opened onto a courtyard. Here Dafydd helped her to dismount, and she stood confusedly watching as the ponies were unladen, and Mr. Glendower, Mrs. Mowbray and Ellen disappeared through the front door.

Dafydd jerked a thumb towards the oldest part of the house. "The kitchen's round there, Matilda. Just make yourself known."

Nervously she picked her way through the mounds of luggage, and stamping ponies, and pushed open an iron-studded door leading to a large, stone-flagged kitchen. Almost an entire wall was taken up by a range on which were saucepans and pans emitting smells which reminded Miranda that she had not eaten a decent meal for hours.

Flitches and hams hung from hooks near the range, and several maids in white aprons and mobcaps hurried in and out of the kitchen. A little scullery maid, in a coarse sacking apron, her arms deep in hot water in one of the sinks, saw Miranda and said something in Welsh. Miranda smiled tremulously as a pale thin woman, with iron-grey hair skewered beneath her lace cap, bustled into the room carrying a jar of preserved peaches.

She addressed the company in loud and rapid Welsh, noticed Miranda and stopped to stare. Then dropping her a curtsy she smiled, and her voice assumed a honeyed tone.

"You've come to the wrong door, miss. What was the

men doing to allow such a thing? Myfanwy, show the young lady to her proper place. Look sharp there, girl, don't stand goggling. What will the master say when he finds that one of his guests . . .?"

"Oh, but I'm not a guest," burst out Miranda. She realised that this must be Mrs. Pritchett, who had it in her power to make her life bearable—or otherwise.

"I . . . I'm not a guest," she repeated. "I'm the new seamstress. I travelled from London with Mrs. Mowbray and Miss Ellen."

All sound ceased, then the scullery maid giggled nervously, and the housekeeper's face became tinged with purple as she looked Miranda up and down.

"You don't act like a seamstress," she snapped.

"I beg your pardon," said Miranda, "but I don't know how a seamstress . . . that is I have never seen one before . . ."

She stopped. Mrs. Pritchett's small slate-coloured eyes bored into hers, then she turned and gave several raucous orders. The maid scuttled back to work, and Mrs. Pritchett beckoned Miranda, who followed her through an inner door. She found herself in a parlour which was small and stuffy with the heat of a big fire and smelled of cooking. Trying to prevent the distasteful wrinkling of her nose, she stood waiting while Mrs. Pritchett seated herself in a wing chair.

"I don't know where Mrs. Mowbray found you," she said vehemently, "but you'd better know, here and now, that your airs and graces don't cut no ice with me, no more than your fancy way of talking does. If you're a servant here, I'll thank you to act like one, and you'll treat me and Mr. Merrick, the butler, with the respect due to our stations."

"Indeed, I had no thought of being anything other than polite," said Miranda. "I think the main party forgot about me, and I didn't know what to do. I don't yet know how I should go on, you see . . ."

"There you go again, setting yourself up to be better than you should. Well, it won't do." The woman's voice became shrill. "And what's more, no one told me to expect another mouth to feed nor a bed to prepare.

26

You'll have to wait till I've time to see to things. Now go and make yourself useful. I reckon you'll not be doing any fancy sewing tonight."

Miranda returned to the kitchen, her eyes blurred with angry tears, and blundered into someone who felt as soft and yielding as a fur rug. She dashed a hand across her eyes as a gentle voice said, "There now, lovey, don't let her upset you. Come over here and peel these mushrooms. Mrs. Glendower has a weakness for them, and I like to give her what she wants, poor soul, she's always ailing.

"I'll get Myfanwy to make you a cup of coffee as soon as Mrs. Pritchett's gone. She'll go upstairs soon and talk to the gentry that smooth I wonder oil don't drip from her chin. I'm Mrs. Rhys, the cook, see, and my trouble is I like my own food a sight too well."

She gave a rumbling laugh, which rippled through her several chins and rotund figure, and Miranda warmed to her with gratitude.

"That's better, then. My, you're even prettier when you smile. Course, you'll not do kitchen work regular, but it's best you occupy yourself now. It'll make you feel more at home."

Sitting down, Miranda began the homely task which she found strangely comforting. "These are very fine," she said, "are they local?"

"Bless you, yes, they come from the home farm. We get our dairy food there. The soil won't grow much but fodder for the animals, but there's nothing like a horse paddock for making mushrooms grow."

She gave her fat chuckle, and Miranda smiled. The coffee was strong and creamy, and Miranda drank it gratefully. Maybe life here would not be so bad, after all.

As soon as family dinner was over, the staff assembled in the servant's hall adjoining the kitchen for their meal. Mrs. Pritchett headed the table, at her left sat a disdainful looking woman, dressed in high fashion, whom Miranda assumed to be a ladies' maid. The rest of the servants sat in descending order of importance, and Mrs. Pritchett ordered that a chair be placed for Miranda immediately above the scullery maid. By now she felt too jaded to care much what happened to her and scarcely

27

noticed the entrance of a tall man in black who took his seat on the housekeeper's right.

Miranda tried to eat the good food before her, but her appetite had failed. All she wanted to do was sleep, and she was startled by a nudge from the little maid beside her.

"They're talking of you."

Miranda looked up the table and saw the senior members of the staff watching her while Mrs. Pritchett spoke in low, fast tones. The man in black gave her a smile, which made her squirm, and Miranda realised that this must be Mr. Merrick, of whom Dafydd had warned her.

"Food not good enough for you?" That was Mrs. Pritchett, and Miranda realised with a shock that she was speaking to her.

"The food is excellent," she replied in the silence which seemed to fall whenever that unpleasant woman raised her voice. "I fear I am too tired to feel hungry."

"The food is excellent," mimicked Mrs. Pritchett, and a sycophantic giggle ran round the table.

Miranda was suddenly angry. She rose to her feet so abruptly that her chair fell over backwards. "I came here," she said in clear tones, "with every intention of working hard and showing respect where I felt it to be due. If I have offended you in some way, then I apologise. It would appear that my duties have not yet been defined, and I should be obliged if someone would have the kindness to show me to my room. I am extremely weary and . . . and need to rest . . . at least for a while."

She knew as soon as she had begun to speak that she had made a mistake. Mrs. Pritchett's eyes, beneath their narrow lids grew even smaller and a look of malice spread over her face. The silence became oppressive. The smell of the cooking, the heat, combined with fatigue, made Miranda turn faint, and she staggered from the table and towards the first door which offered shelter from the goggling eyes.

She was through it before she realised that it was the green baize one leading to the family apartments, but she no longer cared. She simply needed a place to be alone. She hurried through a narrow passage until, hearing voices some way ahead, it occurred to her that Mrs. Mowbray and the others might come upon her. The fear of further caustic comments on her behaviour drove her past coherent thought, and she turned a heavy brass door handle and slipped into the nearest room.

She closed the door and leaned against it, her heart racing, then a distinctive aroma blotted out the immediate present. Leather-bound books! Papa's study, her refuge, when, as a child, she had escaped from her older brothers' and sisters' teasing or the stern commands of her nurse, had this dear familiar scent. She had breathed it as she learned her lessons, and later, copied out Papa's sermons in her fine hand.

She looked about her. The room was lighted only by the fire in a fine marble grate and a bronze oil lamp, which stood on a gilded library table by the fender. A comfortable-looking wing chair was near the table. Miranda's eyes travelled slowly over the volumes which lined the room and the pinewood panelling over the door. The largest piece of furniture was an open Queen Anne bureau, on which were account books and papers, and the floor was carpeted in beaver-brown. The room was sombre, yet restful, and Miranda wondered who could be the scholar. Surely not Gethin Glendower of the worn clothes and arrogant manner.

She realised that the voices had died away at the same time as she heard a brisk step on the stone-flagged hall. Someone was coming! She had better leave quickly! It was too late: the steps approached the door, the handle turned and in unreasoning panic Miranda darted across the room and squeezed herself in a narrow gap left between the side of the tall bureau and the farthest wall from the fireplace.

The door opened, was roughly slammed, as Gethin Glendower strode into the room saying gratingly, "Damn all women! Damn them to hell!"

For a few moments he paced swiftly up and down before flinging himself into the wing chair.

He's going to read, thought Miranda, and already he's bitterly angry. She couldn't stay where she was, but how could she reveal herself? There was silence now, and she ventured to peer cautiously around the edge of the bureau. The master of Ynys Noddfa sat upright in his chair, his hands clenched on the wings, as he stared into the fire. Perhaps he'll fall asleep, thought Miranda. Please God, let him sleep. But what if he didn't? She drew a deep breath. She hadn't done anything so very bad. Maybe if she explained . . . but how to tell her employer that in the first five minutes of her residence she had been rude to the housekeeper and was now hiding in what was obviously the master's private domain?

He moved suddenly, and she started back, disturbing some of the papers so that they slid from the bureau and floated to the floor.

There was a short hesitation, an exclamation of annoyance, before Mr. Glendower rose and crossed the room. He picked up the papers, then stopped, still bending, and Miranda realised with horror that he had seen her. Slowly his eyes travelled upwards, over her crumpled travelling gown, which she had had no opportunity to change, and to her face.

He straightened abruptly. "What the devil . . .?"

"I . . . I am sorry, sir, I came in by mistake."

He stood staring into her face till she felt the colour rise. "So you came in by mistake! And was it a further error which led you to conceal yourself? Who are you, who comes to my house calling herself a seamstress, yet speaks in accents of culture and has manners which pass you as a lady? What are you doing here? There's mischief enough without anyone . . ."

He stopped, his teeth gnawing his lower lip, then he grasped her wrist and pulled her to the fireplace, grabbing an old reading chair as they went, and thrusting her into it. She sat erect against the hard wooden seat as she returned his glare in the light of the lamp he held above them.

"Now tell me the truth. Who are you and what do you want? If you have insinuated yourself here for some base reason of your own . . ."

"I have not, sir. I have explained my circumstances to you. Surely the fact that you employ me does not give you the right to treat me this way!"

30

"My servants obey me or they leave," he rasped, "and not one of them would have the audacity to enter my study, unasked, which anyone would have told you, had you troubled to enquire, is to violate a place sacrosanct to me."

"I am sorry," cried Miranda, "but my fault is unintentional. How could I know what is right and proper in your house?"

"There are those in the kitchen who would enlighten you."

Miranda remembered the goggling eyes and the spiteful Mrs. Pritchett. "I think you are not familiar with your kitchen," she flashed.

In spite of her effort at self-control, her voice cracked a little, and he held the lamp closed to her face. "Has someone been unkind to you?"

Unkind! What was considered kind or otherwise in the world below stairs? If she complained to this man, who seemed so swift to anger, she could make further trouble for herself.

"I was at fault," she said miserably, lowering her lashes. "I do not yet comprehend the ways . . . of kitchens . . . and domestic service."

He was silent for a moment, but she felt his eyes upon her. "You really are here as a servant, aren't you? Poor little Matilda—come down in the world."

His mockery was unendurable. The worry of the past weeks, the long, tiring and uncomfortable journey, which had ended in such undeserved rancour were expressed in her voice as she cried. "Why should you take out your troubles on hurting me? What have I ever done to you?"

His face filled with fury, and his dark eyes glittered. "Have you the impudence to refer to matters which are no concern of yours? And what do you know of my—troubles?"

"You swore when you entered the room," said Miranda. "You had clearly been upset." She felt overcome by weariness. "But you are correct—I should not have spoken as I did. Please—sir—let me go. I . . . I am so very tired . . ."

She had risen to her feet as she spoke, but staggered

and would have fallen had he not grasped her arm. He placed the lamp on the table, but when she tried to free herself he stared into her face, and for an instant she thought a look of compassion broke briefly through his scowl. She decided she must have imagined it as he said roughly, "Now, Miss Matilda, don't try to get away. Whatever your purpose in coming here, it is clear that you are unfit to pursue it tonight. Here—be seated."

She was past resistance as he helped her into the soft, upholstered wing chair, and his hand had reached the bell rope when there was a tap on the door.

At his response Mrs. Pritchett glided into the room. "If you please, sir, and I'm sorry indeed to trouble you, but a woman has arrived with Mrs. Mowbray, and claims to be a seamstress, but she has disappeared. We have searched the house for her and she cannot be found. I fear there may be some mischief afoot. She's a sly creature and insolent with it. I felt you should know."

"No need for alarm, Mrs. Pritchett. The girl is here."

He stepped aside to reveal Miranda, who now clutched the sides of the wing chair as the housekeeper's eyes bored malevolence into her brain.

"I apologise, sir, for her impudence. How dare you push yourself forward in this way! I suppose, sir, she has tried to delude you into thinking her better than she is. She almost caught me with the same trick. I daresay poor Mrs. Mowbray has been nicely gammoned into bringing her here.

"Come with me immediately, Matilda, you shall be shown a lesson in manners! Don't worry, sir, I'll make sure she learns her place."

"And what exactly is her place, Mrs. Pritchett?"

"That's something that remains to be seen, sir, and please don't trouble yourself further on her account."

"But I feel I must. She is not well, you see. Tomorrow will be soon enough to put her to her duties. Did you make a good supper?"

He fired the question at Miranda, who shook her head unthinkingly.

"There you see," cried Mrs. Pritchett, "the truth

isn't in her. She had good victuals set before her as we always do in your house, sir."

"That is true," agreed Miranda, "it is no fault of Mrs. Pritchett's that I could not eat. I am very tired."

Mr. Glendower rubbed his chin thoughtfully. "Yes, I see that you are. Mrs. Pritchett, please send Mr. Merrick in with Cognac and a glass—and some of those little pastries we had at dinner."

"Cognac! For her!"

"Please do as I say and do not presume to argue."

Mrs. Pritchett gave Miranda a look which made her shudder and stalked from the room.

Gethin Glendower chuckled. "She be on her high horse now. She has a great sense of the fitness of things, has our housekeeper."

All very well for you to laugh, thought Miranda, you are not in her power. But she drank the brandy and water gratefully and nibbled some of the food brought by an impassive Merrick.

Mr. Glendower watched her and took the empty plate. "That's better. You have a brighter colour. How very pretty you are!"

Miranda held up her head. "If I were not a servant, you would not make so personal a remark on so short an acquaintance."

He laughed harshly. "But you *are* my servant, are you not. Don't fear, my girl, I have no intentions upon your honour. The sentiments you heard me express as I entered the room came right from here."

He pressed a hand over his heart as he rose and gave her a mocking bow. Merrick came in answer to his pull on the bell rope and was ordered to send someone to show Matilda to her room and to have her luggage sent there.

The little scullery maid arrived, her awe at this unheard of summons shown in the tremor of the hand which held the iron candle-holder. She led Miranda out and back through the servant's hall, where all speech and activity ceased as the two girls hurried to an uncarpeted back staircase. At the top of the house the maid threw open a door, and Miranda entered a room with sloping

33

sides. "You share this with me and Myfanwy. She's a housemaid and my name's Gwennie."

"I share a room!" Somehow Miranda had never thought about it, but now she realised she had assumed she would be given privacy. A stupid notion! She reminded herself that even at the parsonage the two maids had roomed together. But their apartment had been clean and pretty with two beds and sweet-smelling linen. She looked about her now at the furniture, which was of a former age and had evidently been relegated here when it was damaged or shabby. There was little enough of it. A mahogany chest-of-drawers, a washstand with a black and white marble top on which stood a bowl and a chipped jug with a faded rose design, and a sagging iron-frame double bedstead.

"But where do we all sleep?"

"In there, silly." Gwennie waved a hand towards the bed.

"All three of us!"

"Well, it will be now you've come. Don't worry, there's plenty of room, and on cold winter nights we are glad to snuggle together I can tell you."

Miranda stared at the little maid. Her face was kind, but dirty, and she still smelled slightly of onions and grease. Slowly the tears began to trickle down Miranda's cheeks to plop unheeded onto her gown. "I . . . I can't," she wept, "I can't, indeed, I can't . . ."

A look of hostility replaced Gwennie's smile. "Can't what?" she demanded. "Is it that you think you are too good for us? Maybe Mrs. Pritchett is right about you. She says you think you are somebody, when all you are is a sewing girl."

"I'm sorry, Gwennie, I wouldn't for the world hurt your feelings. It is only that . . . that I am so weary . . . that is what makes me cry, but also I . . . I am a poor sleeper and toss and turn so that you and Myfanwy would get no rest." Having begun the reluctant lie she found herself continuing with a fluency born of her feelings of desperate revulsion. "My mama used to say she would tie me to the bed if I didn't lie still. Not one of us would rest at all."

She managed a weak grin, to which Gwennie responded at once. "Oh, if that is all." She bent and pulled from beneath the bed a narrow trundle bed. "You could sleep on this, though it has a straw mattress and is as hard as a board. Mrs. Pritchett won't unlock the linen cupboards tonight, but I'll look for spare blankets for you, and you can have one of ours."

"Oh, Gwennie, how kind you are!"

The maid's grimy face lit with pleasure. "It's all right, Matilda. It's plain to see that you are not really one of us whatever that cat Mrs. Pritchett says. But you'll have to knuckle down, or she'll make it hot for you."

A footman soon followed with Miranda's luggage, and when Gwennie left she unpacked. The two bottom drawers of the chest were empty so she lined them with tissue from her portmanteau and folded her things carefully away. Her heavy cloth cape she hung on a hook behind the bedroom door. She then took the opportunity to give herself a sponge bath, carefully emptying her slops into the bucket beneath the washstand.

Gwennie slipped back with two rather thin blankets, which she said no one was using, and Miranda climbed into the trundle bed curled inside one of the good flannel nightgowns which Mama had insisted upon. She felt thankful to have brought them as they protected her skin from the prickly blankets, but although she was exhausted she could not relax enough to sleep. Myfanwy and Gwennie came to bed sometime later, and when Miranda saw that both girls retired in their petticoats after a cursory wash, she felt thankful that she lay alone. They fell asleep quite quickly after a giggling conversation, and Miranda lay listening to a sound she could not identify. A kind of subdued roaring which came and went on the fitful wind sighing around the eaves. Then she realized that she heard the sea, which flowed around Ynys Noddfa and turned it into an island.

"I'm a prisoner here," she thought. "We are all prisoners here."

Her last coherent memory was that Gethin Glendower had been dressed in an evening suit of impeccable design and cut and that a black pearl adorned his shirt front. His appearance had been at complete variance with her first sight of him, and his moods seemed to alter as much as his way of dressing. He was as unpredictable as a stormy sky . . .

Chapter Three

After what seemed only minutes Miranda was awakened by Gwennie shaking her gently. She groaned. "Is it time to rise already?"

"Not for you, but I thought I'd best call you 'cos they might forget. Servants' breakfast is at seven and it'll not do to be late or you'll go hungry."

"What time is it now?"

"Five o'clock gone. I'll need to hurry. Me and Myfanwy have a lot to do. Fires to light and the kitchen range to tend."

Gwennie's face still held traces of yesterday's grime and last night's rest, but she smiled kindly before she scuttled off. Further sleep was impossible. Miranda felt moderately refreshed and no longer too weary to push to the back of her mind the fact that she appeared to have landed herself in a position in which she would be far from happy, and she gave a wan smile. How Walter would crow if she had to go crawling back to him! That she would never do, she vowed, and she would write and tell him so today. Perhaps if she tried her hardest to offer Mrs. Pritchett the deference which that lady evidently felt to be her due, she might yet find a happy niche in this house.

But when she presented herself for breakfast, dressed in her plainest grey poplin, she saw extreme dislike reflected in the housekeeper's eyes. Before last night, Miranda had never tried to eat beneath the glare of someone who clearly loathed and resented her. Mrs. Rhys was an excellent cook, the porridge served with fresh rich milk was as smooth as cream, and the home-cured ham with eggs smelled and tasted delicious, but Miranda choked on her food and pushed away half-emptied plates.

"*She* don't appear to care much for your domestic skill," said Mrs. Pritchett, addressing the cook in carrying tones.

Once more Miranda was the centre of attention, but this time she simply lowered her eyes and said, "The food is indeed perfect, but my appetite has not . . . not yet recovered from yesterday's tiring journey."

"Hoity toity!" mocked Mrs. Pritchett. "Such a fine lady. Perhaps, Mrs. Rhys, you should have served her ladyship breakfast in bed." She spoke a rapid flood of Welsh and almost everyone laughed, but Mrs. Rhys said, "Don't mind them, dearie, everyone gets a mite of teasing when they first come. You'll be fine."

Miranda gave Mrs. Rhys a smile of warm gratitude as a tide of colour washed over her face, and Mr. Merrick said, "Our little seamstress deigns to honour us with her approval, Mrs. Rhys." But he, too, spoke kindly, and Miranda included him in her glance. Mr. Merrick's bosom swelled, and he favoured her with a leer and a wink, while Mrs. Pritchett, observing the byplay between them, set her thin lips so hard that they almost disappeared.

As soon as the housekeeper had finished, she rose and said, "You will follow me, Matilda."

Wordlessly Miranda was led through doors and passages until they reached a small room which contained a plain wooden table, a straight-backed chair and several large cupboards.

"Here is where you will work. This is the linen which requires mending. When you've done, you'll put it to one side for my inspection. And I warn you that if I'm not satisfied with your work, the stitches will have to come out and the job done again. Is that clear?"

"Yes, perfectly clear, Mrs. Pritchett."

As soon as the housekeeper had left, Miranda examined the high stack of linen. Surely Mrs. Mowbray had said something about a girl kept for plain work, then she shrugged and walked to the window, which was small and latticed like the others in the old part of the house. The sewing room was on the first floor. Below was a kitchen garden sheltered behind a high stone wall over which Miranda could see the ocean. The tide was out, and there was a large expanse of sand, rocks and pools. She wished she could go out to walk, to explore, to run; anything rather than sit in this bare room with its wooden floors to begin some of the most tedious stitching she could imagine. At home she had always done the fine work, and the maids had mended seams and rents, and furthermore, she remembered indignantly, Papa had provided them with a sewing machine. She searched the cupboards but found no evidence of this useful article, so rebelliously she threaded her needle and began the laborious task of repairing the hem of a heavy linen sheet.

She was left in solitude, sewing steadily, occasionally stretching her aching back, until her watch told her that it was past ten o'clock and nearly three hours since Mrs. Pritchett had brought her here. She was regretting that she had not forced herself to eat more and made a firm resolve that no matter what the provocation offered, in future she would not add the pangs of hunger of a healthy appetite to the tedium of her work.

Suddenly the door opened and Gwennie entered, peering back over her shoulder and carefully holding a steaming cup, which she handed to Miranda, who thanked her. "I thought I had been forgotten."

"You 'aven't been forgotten," said Gwennie significantly. "You are only too well remembered by certain people. But the old cat wasn't going to send you any refreshment though she knows, like we all do, that you couldn't eat this morning."

Miranda held her aching fingers round the cup as she sipped the rich cocoa. "But she allowed me to have this —or someone did."

"That they didn't. Mrs. Rhys would've, but Mrs. Pritchett give the order that you was to be left alone. It would bring you to a proper humility is what she said."

"Then how . . .?"

"I was left in the scullery and saw my chance when the kitchen was empty for a minute. People forget me, see. I dashed in and poured this from the pot on the oven range, and I brought these as well." She delved into her apron pocket and withdrew a macaroon. "The new

39

lady, Mrs. Mowbray, ordered them. Seems she's a fancy for them. Mrs. Rhys made a lot so she'll likely not miss one."

Miranda could not hurt the maid's feelings by refusing so she closed her mind to the grime on the apron and the grimy grease on the rough red hand held out to her and ate the macaroon.

She winced at the scalding cocoa, and Gwennie cried, "Don't you be hurrying, miss, you'll burn your throat."

"You must not address me as 'miss,' Gwennie. What would Mrs. Pritchett say?"

"Oh, her! Well, I daresay I'd better not, but you seem like a 'miss' to me. It isn't right and proper that you should have to be treated so bad."

"I was hurrying for your sake. What will happen if you are missed?"

Gwennie grinned, "I'll say I had to pay a call in the yard, if you'll forgive my speaking so, miss, I mean, Matilda. They can only yell at me, or give me a clout, and I'm used to them, so I am."

"How old are you?"

"Twelve or thereabouts, and I've been here for two years and glad to be, I can tell you. It's a sight better than the poorhouse where I was left, and I reckon I'm lucky not to be sent to a factory or a mine."

Miranda finished her cocoa and picked up her needle. Gwennie stared. "You're never doing those hems by hand, are you? Why don't you wait till the machine's repaired?"

"Then there is a sewing machine! I thought its absence strange in so large an establishment."

"Mrs. Pritchett came up here very early and had it took away. She said it needed mending, though I don't remember Ceinwen saying so."

"Ceinwen?"

"She's the regular girl who comes up from the village to do the sewing. She's been away from Wales working, but her granny, who reared her, is sick, and Ceinwen's come back to tend her. Her granny, Mrs. Morgan was seamstress here for years, but now she's not fit, and Ceinwen comes in her place." Gwennie looked at the floor.

40

"Matter o' fact, Matilda, it did seem funny to us that Mrs. Mowbray brought you all the way from London when Ceinwen badly needs the money she earns here, though of course you wasn't to know that."

Miranda flushed. "I had no thought of taking away someone's livelihood, indeed I had not, and Mrs. Mowbray gave me to understand that I would be employed more as a tailoress and instructress to the young ladies."

"Likely you will then. Mrs. Pritchett sent to tell Ceinwen not to come again, but she'll have to change her orders perhaps. I hope so. 'Twould serve the old cat right."

Miranda sighed as Gwennie took her cup. "I hope that I do nothing more, even inadvertently, to upset Mrs. Pritchett. Not one of my words or actions seem to satisfy her, yet I have not tried deliberately to flaunt her wishes. Why is she so unkind to me? Is she so with everyone at first?"

Gwennie paused, stared again at the floor, and mumbled, "Only the pretty ones, and you are the prettiest of the lot."

"But what have my looks to do with her?"

"Well, I'll tell you, since you'll learn soon or late, I reckon. See, she's not a 'missus' at all she's really a 'miss' like yourself. Mr. Merrick says it's what's called a . . . a courtesy title, I think he said."

"Quite right," said Miranda, "but I still don't see . . ."

"She've never been married, and it seems it's what she wants above everything. She was the daughter of a respectable draper, leastways, 'twas thought he was respectable, then it turned out he'd been spending too much money, and not paying his bills, and he went bankrupt. Then he walked out onto the sands in the Mawddach Estuary and waited for the tide to cover him. His missus never got over the shame, and when she got ill with lung fever the next winter she died, too, and Miss Pritchett, as she really is, had to go to work. There's talk that she was about to be betrothed, but nothing came of it. Likely he sheered off when her father was disgraced."

"Well, I'm sorry for her," said Miranda, "but hurting me—how does that help her?"

41

"It's Mr. Merrick. He's a widower and she've had an eye to him for ages, but he likes pretty girls, so she gets rid of temptation. But she've found it easy past times, but you are different 'cos you've been brought special from London, and she don't know how she'll go on now with you. I reckon she'll keep you up here as much as she can."

Miranda felt appalled. She would be like a prisoner. She imagined the lonely hours ahead and asked, "How can she wield so much power? Has the mistress of the house no say in anything—and what of Mr. Glendower?"

"I've hardly ever seen Mrs. Glendower. She've always kept a lot to her room, and now she never leaves it. I think she's ill though no one seems to know what ails her and as for the master—well, things aren't what they might be between them. I've heard Miss Bailey, that's the ladies' maid, telling things to Mrs. Pritchett when they didn't know I was listening. They say . . ."

"That will do, Gwennie, I cannot listen to gossip."

The two girls stared at one another. Miranda had reacted as she would have done in the past to talebearing from a servant, and now Gwennie smiled a little sadly, "See, you *are* different from the rest of us. I'm thinking you'll have a hard time of it, Matilda."

Miranda took both the rough little hands in hers. "Forgive me, dear, I had not meant to be abrupt. Heaven knows, you're the only friend I seem to have at present."

Gwennie gave Miranda's fingers a gentle squeeze. "That's all right. And I suppose I shouldn't repeat talk that wasn't meant for me, but you can't help but see that the master's not happy. Maybe the new lady will make things comfier."

Thinking of Mrs. Mowbray, Miranda had doubts. Life above and below stairs might become more efficiently conducted, but Mrs. Mowbray probably placed more value on economy than comfort, at least for the servants.

At the sound of a heavy tread on the uncarpeted landing, Gwennie looked around wildly. "It's her—Mrs. Pritchett—she'll slaughter me if she catches me here and with this cup besides." Grabbing the empty cup, she darted across the room, pulled open a cupboard door and hurled herself on top of a pile of sheets, clicking the door behind her.

Mrs. Pritchett entered looking about her, "Is Gwennie here?"

"Why would you think she would be?" dissembled Miranda.

"She'll do anything to get out of work, that one, and I can find her nowhere. She'll be gossiping no doubt. Well, she'll be punished."

The housekeeper picked up a pillow case from a pile on the table. "You don't seem to have done much."

"It is very slow work to sew such heavy material by hand. A sewing machine would answer the purpose far better and leave me free for more delicate work."

"Really! It's hardly for you to dictate what we use here." She stalked to the window and stared out at the grey sky. "It's cold for August," she remarked.

Miranda did not reply. Anything she said seemed only to add to Mrs. Pritchett's venom. The housekeeper, still with her back turned said, "You've been sent for upstairs. Apparently Mrs. Mowbray has told some fanciful story about you being able to make real lace like the old stuff, and Mrs. Glendower wants you to show her some. You'd better be able to make good your claim or you'll be in trouble."

"I do not lie, Mrs. Pritchett."

The other woman turned and gave her a look of hatred. "I do not lie," she mocked. "You're lying now just by being here. What right have you to come and pass yourself off as a servant? I suppose you've been thrown onto the world and are looking for a soft landing. Well, you won't find it here, I'll see to that."

"I assure you I have no such thoughts. Please, if I am to go to Mrs. Glendower, will you not show me the way?"

Mrs. Pritchett drew back her chin. "Don't try to give me orders. You'll come to the kitchen, and a maid will take you upstairs."

She walked out and Miranda was able to dart unseen across the room and release the cupboard latch for Gwennie to escape. The door swung open, and the scullery maid stared up at her. She had a corner of a sheet stuffed in her mouth, and her face was a mixture of terror and laughter. Miranda gave her an irresistible grin and sped after Mrs. Pritchett.

A trim parlour-maid waited for Miranda to fetch a sample of lace, then led her through the stone-flagged passages of the old part of the house until suddenly they appeared to step into another world as they entered the hallway of the new extension. Ahead was the door through which Mrs. Mowbray and Ellen had vanished on her first day here, and to the right an elaborately carved newel post guarded a staircase. In every corner was a jardiniere holding a potted plant or a statuette. The gold, green and brown wallpaper matched the fussy design of the carpet.

Miranda followed the maid to the first floor, where she tapped on a door, which was opened by a sulky-looking Miss Bailey, and Miranda entered a room which was filled to claustrophobic point with all manners of objects. Red was the predominant colour. It was in the walls, carpet and curtaining and in the rich pattern of the hangings of the half-tester bed. The slight woman who leaned back into the lace-trimmed pillows seemed to be half lost in a crimson world. So this was Mrs. Glendower, the woman whom Gethin Glendower presumably had included in his blasphemous imprecations. Her face was pale, and her auburn hair, on which was pinned a frilled cap, was without lustre. Around her shoulders lay a white knitted shawl, which she tugged about her with thin, nervous hands as she turned dull-green eyes towards Miranda.

"So you are Matilda." At the gentle sweetness of the voice Miranda wondered even more at the vehemence of her husband's tone.

"Yes madam," she replied, giving a small curtsey. Somehow she didn't mind humbling herself before this serenely courteous lady.

"Mrs. Mowbray tells me that you sew passably well. Those are her words, not mine." Her smile lit her face. "My husband's cousin is not give to extravagant praise. I should so much like to see the lace of which she spoke."

Miranda handed Mrs. Glendower a blouse. "This is somewhat finer than the work I showed Mrs. Mowbray.

I thought you would be better able to judge my ability by it."

Mrs. Glendower touched the lace caressingly. "You are an artist, Matilda." She looked up suddenly, and the green eyes grew keen. "And you are not of the serving class, I think."

There was a snort from the dressing table, where the maid was trying to create order among the chaos of small boxes and bottles.

"You may leave me, Bailey. I will talk a while with Matilda."

Miss Bailey stamped to the door, and as she disappeared Mrs. Glendower chuckled. "She is fiercely jealous, you know. She does not want anyone but herself to hold sway in my room." She patted the bed. "But she is gone now, so sit by me here, my dear, and explain how you come to find yourself in so menial a position."

She listened intently. "So you ran away from your brother because he was trying to marry you to a man you did not care for."

"Yes, madam, I know I have done wrong in the eyes of the world . . ."

"You have done right, Matilda." Miranda was startled by the vehemence of her tone. "Would to God all women had your courage. If only I . . ." Then he stopped, realising perhaps that Miranda was, after all, a seamstress in her house, but her eyes turned to the pictures which jostled for space on the walls and lingered on a framed print. It was incongrous among the original oils and water-colours, but Mrs. Glendower's gaze was intense as she stared at the scene.

"It is a print of 'The Long Engagement' painted by Mr. Arthur Hughes," she murmured. "See the sad face of the girl as she clings to her lover's hand while he turns from her, so stern and unrelenting. Yet she will wait for him. Something tells me that someday they will marry and that she has the courage to wait, as you did, Matilda. She has the determination."

After a short silence Mrs. Glendower reached out and took Miranda's hand in her own, which was hot and dry. "How have you fared with Mrs. Pritchett?"

As Miranda hesitated, Mrs. Glendower continued. "Your silence answers me. I think she is not a kind person. I cannot run the house without assistance, you know, and she is strong—I need her strength." Tears sprang to her eyes. "I ought to be up and about. I know it is my duty to watch over the welfare of my servants, but I cannot, I cannot . . ." Her voice was becoming shrill, and Miranda was alarmed.

"Dear ma'am, don't distress yourself. I am sure that if you are ill no one expects . . ."

"*He* expects—he does not believe—and indeed, I feel he may be right. It may all be due to my nervous state as my husband insists." She began to gasp. "Go to my dressing table, dear, there is some medicine there—it calms me—it is a herbal mixture I have had put up."

Miranda ran to the dressing table and searched among the many items there. Clark's Blood Mixture, Bunter's Nervine, Scott's Bilious and Liver Pills, breath sweetener, tooth whitener, Pulmonic Wafers, the supply of medicaments seemed endless, yet she could not find anything resembling a herbal mixture. The gasping from the bed grew frantic, and in her agitation Miranda was unaware that the door had opened until she heard a voice. "You are hysterical, Lora. Control yourself. Where is Bailey? Why are you attended only by the seamstress?"

Gethin Glendower stood with his back to the closed door, a frown on his lined face. Miranda looked at Lora, who seemed even paler. "I am not well, Gethin, my love, truly I am not, and Matilda cannot find . . ."

Striding across the room he jerked open the door of the bedside cabinet and took out a bottle. "Why pretend, Lora," he said harshly, "Give me a glass, Matilda, my wife's most-used medicine is here, marked Cognac." He poured a measure and, without adding any form of dilution, put the glass into Lora's shaking hand. "Drink it down, my dear, it will do you good."

If he spoke so to me, thought Miranda, I would fling the drink in his face, but Lora held the glass to her trembling lips, and Miranda realised with pity that the sick woman was well used to the fiery liquid and to the irritation which her craving caused her husband.

Gethin Glendower turned sharply to stare at her. "You look astonished, Miss Seamstress. When we are all better acquainted, you will not be, I promise you."

Miranda had forgotten her position long enough to open her mouth to fling him an angry retort, but the words were stifled unborn as she saw that underlying the anger in her employer's expression was a wretchedness which devastated her, and made her wonder which of these two stood more in need of compassion. Especially when Lora finished her drink and spoke almost serenely, as if nothing had happened. "Gethin, I have been talking to Matilda and have seen her skilled work. I was wondering, now that Angharad's latest governess has left, if she could not teach sewing and perhaps other crafts to our daughter."

He answered coolly. "You are at liberty, madam, to engage Matilda in whatever capacity you wish. Let us hope that she will have more success in her endeavours than have the others."

He strode out of the room and closed the door resoundingly behind him. Mrs. Glendower held a hand to her head and groaned. "I think I have one of my headaches approaching. Matilda, do you play the pianoforte?"

"Why, yes, Mama educated us in all the accomplishments."

"See over there, I have had my little upright brought here. I have many of my treasures about me now I can no longer go downstairs. My illness has become suddenly so much worse. Could you play to me a little? I should be so grateful."

Miranda looked at the sheet music, which was scattered over the pianoforte in the reckless profusion which seemed to encompass everything in the room. She rejected Dance Music and ten songs by Mr. Arthur Sullivan and settled for Brahm's Piano Album. Her fingers drew music from the instrument with real talent, and when she had finished Lora was lying back with closed eyes. She spoke softly, "That was delightful, my dear." The green eyes flew open. "You heard my husband give his permission for me to engage you in whatever way I desire—I did not imagine it. Will you help me, Matilda, and my poor little daughter? Will you sew for us and play your music and be a companion?

"Come here to me. You have a kind face, Matilda. You are very pretty, but kindness is more important. Could you find it in your heart to be patient with a poor invalid and her somewhat wilful child? My little Angharad has not had the training she should. She has driven all her governesses away, but she needs a friend so desperately. Could you be that friend, do you think?"

Miranda took the fragile hand between her own strong ones. How could Gethin Glendower have spoken so cruelly to his wife? Had he no pity? "I will be as you ask to the best of my ability," she breathed.

The door was flung open and into the room, like a gale, swept Mrs. Mowbray. "Gethin tells me you are hysterical, Lora. It will not do, you know it simply will not do. I am here to make you see that your indispositions will not be helped by pandering to them unnecessarily. Your condition can only be worsened by undue emotion. You must begin by exercising self-control. Who is that by your bed? The room is so dark with these heavy curtains."

She pulled back the red velvet, allowing light to flood through the net curtaining. "There, that is better." Lora covered her eyes with her hand. "The light makes my head ache, Augusta."

"Nonsense! Oh, it's the seamstress, isn't it? I see you have brought some of your handiwork. What think you, Lora. Is not she a very fair hand at sewing?"

"Very fair," agreed Lora meekly. "And Augusta, did you know that Matilda plays the pianoforte extremely well? Now that the governess has departed, do not you think that Matilda could teach my little Angharad how to sew and play?"

"Someone should teach your little Angharad some manners. She has not spoken to me with due deference. I ordered her to read her primer and she defied me, saying she was going walking. A fine way for a young lady to be reared, I must say."

Lora shrank back into her pillows. "I know, Augusta, but I hope that now you are here . . ."

"You may be sure that I shall instil better ways into her.

48

And your house is disgracefully run! I have had time to make only a cursory inspection, but I tell you, Lora, that I intend to organise your domestics to a much sterner regime.

"And I have already engaged Matilda with a view to her doing more than wasting her time on fancy sewing. In fact," she turned to Miranda, "you will please go to my room and take the velvet dinner gown you will find on my bed. It has become crumpled, and I desire to wear it this evening."

"Cannot your maid do that?" Lora surprised them both by her protest.

"I have dismissed my maid, Lora. I well know that you had a houseful of servants, and when I met Matilda I decided that she could give some of her time to me. And Miss Ellen will need you, too, Matilda. Now you may go."

Miranda dropped a curtsey and turned to leave. On impulse she glanced back. Mrs. Mowbray was holding the bottle of Cognac and tutting loudly. Lora lay back, eyes closed, her face waxen, and Miranda recalled what Papa had taught her of Egyptian tombs. Lora could have been an ancient queen laid to rest, surrounded by the treasures which would sustain her in the life to come.

Outside she looked about her at the several closed doors and wondered which was Mrs. Mowbray's. She was deciding between returning to Mrs. Glendower's room or finding a maid to ask, when a door down the passage opened a little way and a child peered out. Her face was alight with mischief, but when she saw Miranda she scowled. "Who are you?"

"I'm the new seamstress—and you, I think, must be Miss Angharad."

"You are not another horrid governess sent to plague me?"

"Certainly not, and I would be obliged if you could direct me to Mrs. Mowbray's room. I have a task to perform for her, and I have no idea . . ."

The child darted along the corridor, seized Miranda's hand and dragged her into her room. "You needn't bother with that old hag for a while. Come and talk to me—if you're sure you are not a governess."

This child was clearly Lora Glendower's. All the realisation of beauty, which Lora's sickness had ruined, was fulfilled here. Angharad was exquisitely lovely with a perfect creamy complexion, luminous green eyes and hair which tumbled unkempt in rich auburn curls. Her room was as light as Lora's was dark. The pretty carved bed with buttoned padding matched the curtains, and the furniture was of golden satinwood. The two rooms resembled each other only in their disorder and automatically Miranda walked to the washstand to set upright the ewer, which was lying on its side and in imminent danger of falling.

"Leave it!" commanded Angharad. "Let it break. I hate its silly yellow roses. If it falls then Mr. Glendower will have to buy another.

"What do you think of Mr. Glendower? Is not he a handsome fellow? I think all the ladies in the neighborhood must be in love with him."

"You should not speak to me of your father in such a way!"

"Why not, miss seamstress, will you tattle in the kitchen? You could not spread more gossip than is already there, I think."

Miranda's answer was never made. Angharad appeared to lose interest in the conversation and darted across the room and jerked aside a curtain, which had been draped over the front of an open-shelved cupboard. Standing or lying on the shelves were a number of dolls dressed in costumes of various periods.

"How lovely!" Miranda's exclamation drew a chuckle from the child.

"Especially this one, don't you think?" she asked. "Has it not a look of dear Cousin Augusta?"

Miranda felt a little sick. The doll, in the dress of a lady of the court of Marie Antoinette, did indeed bear a resemblance to Mrs. Mowbray, but what riveted Miranda's attention was the long hat pin stuck viciously into the soft body.

"I thought I would try what witchcraft could do." The child's face was distorted by malice. "Ceinwen Morgan's granny is rumoured to be a witch—did you know that?

You have stolen Ceinwen's position, and they are very poor. Perhaps even now Mrs. Morgan is sticking pins into your effigy. Do you feel any pain, seamstress? If you do, will you tell me? I would like to believe that my efforts to rid us of my interfering relative would work."

Miranda snatched the doll from the shelf and, tearing out the pin, dashed it to the floor.

She expected an outburst of rage, but Angharad laughed delightedly.. "My governesses would never have dared do that. You are different. Come, I'll show you dear Cousin Augusta's room. Later you can help me to dress another doll. The stupid woman who has just left did some of these. Tell me if there is someone you hate, and we'll make a matching doll and you shall stick pins into it."

She did not wait for an answer, but ran along the corridor, followed more slowly by Miranda. "That's the room you want. I'm going for a walk."

Miranda watched her race out of sight, her tangled curls flying out behind her. However much she might deprecate Mrs. Mowbray's methods, there was no doubt that some strong hand was needed to set this house to rights.

Chapter Four

Mrs. Mowbray's room was as neat as her person. Miranda picked up the velvet gown from the bed and made her way back to the old part of the house, where she located the kitchen with difficulty. To her relief Mrs. Pritchett was absent, and Mrs. Rhys directed her. "You'll want the laundry, bach. Gwennie, show Matilda the way."

The little maid scuttled out, and Miranda followed her to an outbuilding from which great clouds of steam were issuing. Coal-heated wash boilers bubbled, two women bent over stone sinks up to their elbows in hot suds, and another was turning the huge wooden rollers of a mangle. Gwennie said something to them in Welsh and led Miranda on to a small inner room where a fire burned in a stone hearth.

"You'll find all you need here, Matilda. There's a kettle and pans, see, and box irons on the table, and the goffering frame is over there. Can you manage now?"

Miranda thanked her, and she darted away. She always seemed, thought Miranda, to have too much to do. After refurbishing the gown with boiling water and ammonia, she returned it to Mrs. Mowbray's room. She met no one except maids and seemed to have been forgotten. She looked wistfully through the bedroom window. The sky had cleared and was deliciously blue with small puffs of clouds. A warm sun shone, and the rather scrubby trees in the enclosed garden shook slightly in a soft breeze. Miranda felt hot from her labours in the laundry and stifled by the atmosphere. She did not stop to consider, but knew only that more than anything on earth she wanted to be outside. She was fortunate in meeting no one who could order her movements, and she slipped daringly through the main front door. The salty air invigorated her as she hurried to the beach and scrambled over boulders in their shell and pebble beds until a bend took her out of sight of the house. Now the sand was smooth beneath her thin shoes, and she strode beside the waves to the high dunes.

Holding up her skirts she climbed, laughing as her feet slipped in the steep sand, until she reached the top and stared in wonderment. She was looking down into a green bowl of vegetation formed by the encircling dunes. An oyster catcher flew into the air screaming its alarm call, and a rabbit darted into a burrow. Flowers grew in profusion and as she half climed, half slid, down into the bowl, she almost could taste the heavy-scented air.

At the bottom of the hill she sat down and spread her skirts about her, revelling in the unexpected peace and beauty. Her stillness encouraged the larks, which had followed the oyster catcher, to return twittering to their ground nests.

She held her breath as a rabbit appeared and hopped closer to her, but it darted away, and once more the birds rose, protesting, into the sky. She realised what had disturbed them when Gethin Glendower came sliding down the dunes on the other side of the hollow. Miranda looked quickly about her, but there was no way she could escape unnoticed. Perhaps if she stayed motionless, he would not see her. She watched him as he strolled nearer. The harsh expression on his face had vanished; he looked contented as he walked slowly closer, sometimes stopping to examine a plant, once laughing at a family of rabbits which bobbed away almost under his feet. Then the laugh died abruptly, and Miranda realised she was discovered. His face set into its usual stern lines as he approached, and Miranda rose.

They stared at one another for a brief space until Miranda felt compelled to say, "I should not be here. I ... escaped ..."

"Escaped! From my house?"

She flushed. "That was impolite of me. I merely meant to say that I had run from duties which I found . . .

53

found somewhat tedious. I am sorry. It won't happen again."

She turned to leave, but paused as his voice, more gentle than she would have believed possible, said "Look at this flower, Matilda, before you go. Is it not beautiful?"

In his hand he held a tiny purple and white wild orchid, and she exclaimed with delight. He spoke softly, "Somehow I knew that you would care for it. My family, in general, seem to favour the hot-house blooms, but I find them showy, do you not agree, Matilda?"

When she did not answer, he said, "Of course, you are not at liberty to criticise your employers, are you? Quite right. How discreet you are. I suppose it comes of being a parson's daughter."

"I did not tell you that."

"No more you did, but when my wife suggested that you should, in some measure, be a friend to Angharad, I questioned Mrs. Mowbray more closely about you. It seems that you act on impulse, Matilda. You have left your brother's protection, taken a position you are ill-qualified to fill . . ."

"I am an expert needlewoman!"

"So are many other ladies. They do not all desire to gain a living by it, which is fortunate. If half the staff were the sons and daughters of gentlemen, it would be impossible to direct the household. I meant that you are ill-qualified by temperament and not by skill. I should be surprised indeed to find any others of the domestics sitting in the sun admiring the view at a time when they should be about their duties."

Colour flared in Miranda's cheeks. "Once more, I beg your pardon, sir. I will return at once."

"There is no escape from them, Matilda, you will discover, as I have—to my cost. You must do your duty in the capacity to which God has called you, Matilda." He laughed harshly as, with an impatient cry, she lifted her skirts and tried to hurry away.

She heard his laughter as she struggled. "Lesson number two—you cannot run up a sand dune. Impulsive Matilda . . ."

She fled back to the house, too cross to remember

Mrs. Pritchett until she hurried through the kitchen door. The housekeeper was waiting, her narrowed eyes grey flints as she gave Miranda the full benefit of her tongue. "How dare you walk out of the house during your hours of duty. I would punish you . . . I wish I could punish you . . ." She stopped, almost choking on her rage. "Mrs. Mowbray wishes to see you. She has been waiting for over half an hour."

Miranda hastily smoothed her hair and dusted down her gown. Her shoes were full of sand, but she dared not take time to empty them now, and she followed Mrs. Pritchett from the room.

Mrs. Mowbray was seated at her dressing table, her hair unbound. "Ah, thank you, Pritchett. You may go."

The housekeeper stalked out, and Miranda waited. Mrs. Mowbray ignored her while she pinned a brooch into the boned collar of her black silk gown and eased an onyx ring onto her finger. "I need help with my hair. Have you any skill in that direction, Matilda?"

Miranda silently took the hair brush. At that moment she felt that Mrs. Pritchett's open hostility was easier to bear than this woman's careless disregard of any finer feelings she possessed. "I am accustomed to attending to my own, madam, and I dressed my Mama's," she said, as she began to brush the iron-grey hair.

"I suppose you would need to do so. Your Papa's living was a poor one, I gather. Had he no influential frends to help him?"

"Certainly he had! Also there were members of our own family who desired him to take one of the rich livings to be had, but my Papa was a fine man who went where he was most needed. He loved the poor folk. All the spare money we had went to help those less fortunate than ourselves. I would not have wished it any other way."

"I daresay. And I suppose he had many offspring. I have often observed that poor parsons generally do."

Miranda clung to the shreds of her temper. "I have three brothers and four sisters, madam."

"As I suspected! Why did you not go to one of them for shelter in your need? Have you quarrelled with them all?"

"Indeed not! I do not wish to be a burden to any of them. Not one is rich in worldly goods, and *they* do not think material possessions to be of first importance."

"Matilda! Do not speak to me in so vehement a fashion. and do not tug my hair. It is not for you to argue with your betters. I have every right to make any comments I choose."

She stared into the mirror, and their eyes met. "I wonder if you are suitable, after all, to be trusted in close proximity with my young Cousin Angharad. She requires a steadying influence."

Miranda drew Mrs. Mowbray's hair back and pinned it deftly into a chignon, then took a deep breath. "I apologise, madam, if I have been too outspoken. I love my family and I loved and admired my father and have not been used to curb my tongue. Indeed, he himself often reproached me for being declamatory, but I feel I must defend the memory of one who was so good and kind. I have met Miss Angharad briefly. Her behaviour seems unrestrained, and for that very reason I feel I might understand her better than her governesses seem to have done. I do not feel qualified to undertake much academic instruction, but I would try to be a companion to her and perhaps impart some of my skills."

There was a long silence. Mrs. Mowbray lifted a hand mirror and examined her hair from all angles. "This is well done, Matilda. You are clearly going to be useful to me. By the way, I have given orders that the sewing girl is to return to work. You will do only fine sewing between your duties with me and the young ladies." She consulted her fob watch before pinning it to her bosom. "You had better return to the servants' quarters or you will miss your meal."

Downstairs, Gwennie, her arms immersed in hot soda water as she washed dishes, stared round at Mrs. Pritchett, whose eyes gleamed as she declared, "It's not a bit of use coming late to your dinner, Matilda Courtney. It is served at twelve o'clock—no earlier and no later—and now we are busy with upstairs lunch to see to, so you'd better be about your duties. I suppose you can find your way back to the sewing room."

Miranda's anger boiled over. "That is unjust! Unfair, Mrs. Pritchett. I was kept by Mrs. Mowbray. I am sure that Mrs. Glendower would not have her servants treated so were she able to order her household."

"Now, now, it's all right, ladies. I realised, Mrs. Pritchett, that you had forgotten to keep Matilda a bite so I ordered a dish to be kept hot for her."

Mrs. Pritchett whirled as Mr. Merrick's voice came from behind her. "You did what?"

Mr. Merrick eyed the housekeeper. "I did what you always do for a maid kept at her duties, and what I'm sure you meant to do. You simply don't have time for everything."

Mrs. Pritchett answered him with a flood of Welsh while her colour came and went. Mr. Merrick's answer was smooth, and he ended by taking her hand and patting it. Myfanwy tugged at Miranda's skirt. "Here, bach, come and eat. He's just telling her how wonderful she is. Get this food down you before she notices."

Miranda sat at a corner of the kitchen table and, remembering her resolve, ate rapidly while the servants bustled about her. Mrs. Rhys, red-faced and shrill, directed the final touches to the lunch. If it had not been for the housekeeper's hostility, Miranda could have found her new life absorbing. She had sometimes eaten in grand houses and had had no idea of the ordered turmoil which ended in the calm serving of meals to the master and his family and guests.

She took her empty plate to Gwennie and Mr. Merrick, who waited to lead the procession of maids and footmen to the dining room, gave a quick look about him, saw that Mrs. Pritchett was absent and hurried to Miranda's side. "You got our good housekeeper properly set against you then, haven't you? But don't worry, little girl. I'll look after you."

Miranda tried not to shrink away as he patted her shoulder. He moved hastily from her as the housekeeper entered and glared at them. Miranda shivered. She felt she could not have borne the atmosphere in the kitchen a moment longer as she made her way to the sewing room and seating herself at the table, resumed her laborious work.

The remainder of the day was uneventful. Miranda, her fingers sore from handling the heavy materials, her back and head aching, hoped that someone would send for her. When hours passed, broken only by meals in the servant's hall, where she was glared at silently by Mrs. Pritchett, she began to think that she had been forgotten. Decisions could be made upstairs, she realized, which affected her deeply, yet she need never know what had been proposed and discarded. Was she doomed, after all, to spend her days cooped up here alone in this bare room, her skills unwanted?

That night she retired early and lay in her hard bed trying to read in the failing light from the small dormer window. The waves sounded louder, though there was no wind. Soon after dark Myfanwy and Gwennie came to bed, and Miranda pretended to be asleep. Their conversation was in Welsh; once she heard the name "Matilda," but she felt unequal to talking to them.

Gradually her inner turmoil calmed, and she slept. The sound of the wind awoke her. It screamed and whined about the rooftops like a thousand demons, and there was a roar like the sound of a train. She sat up abruptly. Gwennie said drowsily, "Go back to sleep, Matilda. It's only a storm."

"But it was so calm!"

"Calm? Yes, so it was, but the waves were high. That tells of strong winds far out. Now they've reached us. Don't worry, bach, this house was built for storms worse than this."

Miranda lay listening to the fury outside. She had enjoyed wild weather at home, and it had been nothing for her and Papa to go walking over the fields and hills to return, soaked and breathless, to a loving scolding from Mama.

She climbed cautiously out of bed. Gwennie and Myfanwy did not stir, and Miranda dressed herself quickly and took her cloak from the nail behind the door.

The kitchen door was locked and bolted, but the key was there, and Miranda let herself out. As she left the shelter of the courtyard and climbed the short rise leading to the beach, the wind hit her like a physical blow, and she gasped and held on to her cloak. The rain began to lash down, her hood fell back, and her hair, torn from its restraining ribbon, whipped her face in soaked strands.

Miranda laughed aloud. Ever since she had arrived at Mrs. Gash's Registry, she had been forced to hold herself in check. Whatever she said or did annoyed someone, but here there was only the wind and rain and below her the waves, following one upon the other to smash upon boulders and shingle. The turbulent storm, which could be so terrible an enemy, found an echo in her spirit.

She ran, fighting the wind, to where the sea foamed and boiled at her feet, then she turned and struggled along the beach, running when the wind died for an instant, gulping down breath in the strong gusts.

Her body was soaked as the cloak flew about her like huge dark wings; she tripped over a rock and almost fell, when strong arms caught and held her. She began to struggle. "Let me go," she cried against the screaming wind, "Let me go."

"If I did, poor little Matilda might fall. I saved you."

"Mr. Glendower, what are you doing out here . . .?"

They were forced to shout, but above even the noise of wind and waves, she heard his laugh ring out. "This is mine, miss seamstress—and I have the right to be here! But you should be tucked into your cosy little bed like the other menials.

"Only you are not! You are here, as I am, revelling in fighting the simple forces of nature, are you not. We have absconded."

He released her arms and, grabbing her by the hand, dragged her along with him. She was caught up in recklessness, and her laughter joined his as they ran. At last he stopped, and they stood side by side, panting and staring at the rise and fall of the sea.

The rain was fitful now as the clouds scudded across the moon, and Miranda looked up into Gethin Glendower's face. He was watching her, and his strong white teeth flashed in a brilliant smile. As if seduced by their capitulation to the power of the storm they found they were in each other's arms. Their lips met, and Miranda tasted the salt spray in the kiss from the searching mouth on hers.

They broke apart, and he laughed again. But for her the magic was destroyed, and she shrank from him. How could she have behaved with such wanton recklessness? She looked wildly about her. The rain had stopped, and the moon formed a glinting path far out to sea, and painted the drenched boulders a gleaming hue, struggled towards the dunes. Maybe she could hide from him there.

She reached the top and half slid, half fell, into the shelter beyond. Here she was shielded from the worst of the wind, and she began to run. It was useless. She could hear his feet behind her, coming closer, until once more he caught her and held her firmly about the waist. She clenched her fists and struck at him, but he pinned her arms until, helpless, she stood gasping in the grip of one iron-hard arm while his hand stroked her soaked hair from her face.

"Let me go," she begged, "please don't . . ."

"Don't what, poor little seamstress, caught out in the storm by the wicked Sir Jasper? And I have dominion over this island, have I not? I am master here. Who would believe your story when you tried to explain that you were simply out walking in the rain—a demure little sewing girl—when you were set upon and kissed—or worse—by your employer? After all, where would one expect to find a maidservant on such a night as this?"

She tried to struggle, but she was helpless. "Have you no honour, sir?"

"Oh, Matilda, that hurts." His voice was mocking, and the moon was bright enough for her to catch the amusement in his eyes. "Of course I have honour. Do not fear for your virtue—you have no need."

He released her, and he put out a hand as she swayed. She could escape now, but she stayed, staring into the lined face of her employer.

"You are very unhappy," she said, wonderingly. "You possess much, but you are unhappy."

His rage alarmed her afresh. "How dare you presume to criticise me! Especially since you, it appears, have nothing, and take advantage of my money to make your-self a home here."

Miranda's sudden fury matched his own. "A home! Is that what you call this place? Perhaps if you cared enough for people, you would try to discover what sort of . . . of hell-hole your servants enjoy! I may be only a serving maid, sir"—here, she dropped him a curtsey—"but in my papa's house, which was humble compared with yours, we gave our maids good beds and made fair rules for the benefit of all. He would not have expected me to travel in acute discomfort and to exist in my present conditions."

"Travel in discomfort! You travelled first class. Why, I saw you leave the compartment. Is not that enough for you? Did you desire that I should send the family coach for you? And I have no personal knowledge of your sleeping quarters, but I do know that we have rooms enough for you to be comfortable, whatever your status."

"Indeed! Well, I had not meant to speak out, but now I will say that apart from the last few miles, I travelled apart from the others on my journey here, and my quarters are . . . are worse than at Mrs. Gash's Servant's Registry. And I am expected to do the work of several different domestics and to suffer hunger through no fault of my own. At least I would if your odious butler had not rescued me!"

He gripped her wrist until she cried out. "Odious? What has Merrick done?"

"Nothing! Oh, nothing, I assure you. Please release me. He made sure I ate when the housekeeper said I was too late. But he . . . he . . ." How could she make him comprehend a fear which was too tenuous to put into words. "He is odious, that is all."

He stood motionless, staring down at the sand. The storm was dying, and she could hear the couch grass as it danced and rustled in the breeze. She realised suddenly that she was chilled, and she shivered as the wind seemed to slice through her wet clothes.

"You're cold, Matilda."

He began to walk towards the house, and she followed. He's impossibly arrogant, she thought. He leads and everyone trails after him, yet still she walked in his footsteps. What else was there to do? Without warning he stopped and waited for her. A few feathers of wind-tossed cloud turned the moon into a flickering lantern as he demanded, "Who in God's name called you Matilda? Had your parents no sense of what fitting? Even as a baby I cannot imagine you as anything but beautiful!"

Her suppressed irritation at Mrs. Mowbray was unleashed. "Your cousin re-christened me. Mama and Papa would never have given me that name."

"Augusta changed your name?"

"Yes, and now I suppose you will tell me that you are innocent of the fact that your servants can ever be re-named to suit their employers!"

He ignored her rudeness. "What *are* you called?"

"Miranda, if you must know. Papa's favourite play was . . ."

"*The Tempest*, of course." He laughed. "Miranda of *The Tempest*. Now I understand everything. Are you always drawn to storms, Miranda? Are you not afraid that you may meet a Caliban? Or maybe you think that tonight you did."

They had almost reached the house, and his laughter followed her as she sped round to the kitchen door and let herself in. The long sleeves and high neck of her heavy cotton dress clung uncomfortably to her skin and, after hesitating nervously, deciding that no one would enter the kitchen again so late at night, she removed it. She stood in the warmth from the banked-up range, shivering, before she wrung out what water she could from her dress, cloak and petticoat skirts into the sink. She wished she dared leave her garments by the fire to dry, but the thought of Mrs. Pritchett deterred her. Her excitement had died, and she felt utterly weary. Even her trundle bed held a welcome. She threw her damp cloak about her shoulders and, holding her dress over her arm, turned to go. Then her heart thudded as she realised that someone in a dressing gown barred her way. It was Merrick!

Pulling her cloak tightly about her, she stared at him. His eyes travelled slowly up and down her body and came to rest on the dress she held. He smiled and Miranda could not repress a shudder. His gaze seemed to penetrate her clothing. He began to approach her, and she stood her ground. "I . . . I am sorry to have disturbed you, Mr. Merrick. I . . . I felt restless. I have been walking in the rain."

He licked his lips. "I wish I'd known that then, Matilda, I would like to have been with you. But you're here now, aren't you. I've been wanting a little private chat with you."

"I am extremely tired. I really would prefer to retire."

"Would you now? It seems our good Mrs. Pritchett has written you in her bad books, and you'd be wise to take me as a friend. I could be of great service to you. And in return you only have to show me some kindness now and then."

On his last words he stepped nearer and put his hands upon the cloak and tugged. Miranda held it fast. "Let me go. Please, Mr. Merrick, allow me to go."

"Not I! And there's no one to hear you. Only Mrs. P. and I have our quarters near the kitchen, and she'd sleep through the last trump."

With a frantic effort Miranda flung aside his hands and stood straight. "Release me instantly!"

All the breeding of centuries was in her voice and bearing, and instinctively he jumped back. Then dark colour flooded his face. "You little . . . who in hell do you think you are then, coming here with your la-di-da ways and ordering me about? You could have twisted me round your little finger, if you'd shown any sense, but I'll have what I want. I'll . . ."

"So!" The voice which interrupted him was sharp with spite. "So this is what goes on when you supposed I'm asleep." Mrs. Pritchett looked at Miranda with hatred. "I saw you go out, and I watched you come back. You hussy! I knew you were up to no good!"

"I went for a walk, that's all. I love storms—I always have—cannot you understand? I did not expect to find anyone here."

"And in your petticoat, too," the housekeeper said, as if Miranda had not spoken. "Showing him your lovely handmade lace, were you? We'll see what Mrs. Mowbray has to say to this episode. Go to your room. You disgust me." Miranda stood her ground, her face paper white.

"You would not dare to speak to me in that fashion had I anyone to protect me. And you"—she turned to Merrick —"you know that I am innocent of any wrong doing. If I disgust you, Mrs. Pritchett, you nauseate me! Tell Mrs. Mowbray your lies! I have done nothing of which I need be ashamed."

She pushed past the two servants and raced to her room. Myfanwy and Gwennie slept, huddled together. One of them snored a little. The window was sealed against the storm, and Miranda stood with her back to the closed door, loathing the stuffy room. Tomorrow she had no doubt she would be told to leave, and at this minute she did not care. Anything would surely be better than having to live among such people; than having to exist in such conditions.

Weary now beyond belief, she slipped off her under-garments and pulled on her nightgown. She lay sleepless for a long time, reviewing the events of the evening.

When Mrs. Mowbray had heard Mrs. Pritchett, she would have to tell Mr. Glendower. And what would he think? She had returned his kiss. He did not know her. Would he believe her capable of giving way to any man who demanded her caresses? Another memory stirred her. He had called her "beautiful." He thought her beautiful. Why should she care so much what he thought? He was rude, aggressive, domineering, a bully to those about him; in fact all she deplored in a man. Yet suddenly she knew that more than anything she did not want to be turned out of Ynys Noddfa. She abominated him, but she was fascinated by him. Her ideal had always been her gentle, unworldly papa, and Mr. Glendower had seemed to sneer at him. But he stirred her senses as no other man had. And tomorrow it seemed she would be labelled impure, and she would be ordered to pack her bags and go away. But I won't, she decided. I may have to leave in the end, but he shall hear my side of what happened, which will be the truth, if I have to camp out in the dunes and wait to tell him!

Chapter Five

Miranda presented herself in the kitchen for breakfast after a restless night which left her pale and heavy eyed. Gwennie had only spoken to wake her, and no one else addressed her until Miranda left for the sewing room, when the little scullery maid whispered, "Mrs. Pritchett says we are not to talk to you. She says you're a wicked woman."

Her eyes were wide with curiosity, but the small grubby face was troubled, and Miranda gave her a wan smile. "Don't believe all you hear of me, Gwennie."

In the bare sewing room she sat at the table and buried her head in her arms. Her overwrought nerves forced unwilling tears to her eyes. She heard no one enter and jumped when a hand touched her shoulder. It was Myfanwy, who said tonelessly, "You're to go straight to Mrs. Mowbray. I'm to take you." Her reserve broke. "Oh, Matilda, what is it you've done? Mr. Merrick and Mrs. Pritchett aren't speaking to each other, and both of them have boxed Gwennie's ears and she's done nothing to deserve it and Mrs. Mowbray hasn't even had her breakfast yet. Mrs. Pritchett went to her before she was properly dressed, Miss Bailey says, but she was sent away and couldn't tell us more."

Miranda smiled faintly at Myfanwy. "I daresay you will hear all too soon. Perhaps I had better not keep Mrs. Mowbray waiting."

Mrs. Mowbray sat at her dressing table. "Come and dress my hair, Matilda. That tiresome Miss Bailey asserts that she is too busy attending my Cousin Lora to maid me, but you have a way with it."

65

Miranda began to wield the brush, but in her agitated state she twice bumped Mrs. Mowbray's head. The second time the annoyed woman snatched the brush from her. "For heaven's sake, girl. I suppose you have been told that Mrs. Pritchett has been to me almost before my eyes were opened with some story of you and Merrick in the kitchen last night in your . . . your undergarments. I cannot think what possessed the woman to say any such thing—I feel sure there has been a mistake. I do not care for her at all. She has not kept the household in a way I think proper, and my brief examination of the accounts shows discrepancies for which she will be called to answer."

For the first time since last night Miranda felt hopeful. She had not reckoned on support from this quarter, and even if it were only Mrs. Mowbray's dislike of the housekeeper which had prompted it, she had no doubt that Mr. Glendower's cousin must have more influence with him than Mrs. Pritchett.

She stood with her eyes downcast. "I *was* in the kitchen quite late last night. I had been walking in the storm. My clothing became soaked and I removed my gown to wring out the water. Mr. Merrick heard a noise and . . . and rightly came to investigate. I had on my cloak and he wore his dressing gown, but Mrs. Pritchett arrived and drew a conclusion which was utterly false."

Mrs. Mowbray frowned. "Walking! In such a storm! What extraordinary conduct. Yet your behaviour in that line does not warrant dismissal. But I must speak with Mr. Glendower because if I do not then Mrs. Pritchett will have matters all her own way. She ranted on at tedious length about you being a licentious influence in the kitchen. Now continue with my hair, Matilda. You will be informed of the outcome of our deliberation."

Miranda completed the task, and Mrs. Mowbray said, "After Miss Ellen has breakfasted I wish you to go to her room and take her precise measurements. There are several garments she needs."

Miranda left in a daze. Was this a typical servant's life? She was never sure of what was expected of her or where she should be. And Mrs. Mowbray behaved as

66

though last night's incident were merely a bothersome trifle—which to her it probably was. She walked to the sewing room vowing, "If ever I have servants I will endeavour to act with sympathy towards them."

But struggling with the heavy linen she realised how small a chance she had in a world which was so favourable for men and so cruel to a solitary woman. Far from employing servants there seemed every likelihood that she would always be one herself. If not here, then in some sweat shop. Perhaps she would grow frail and fearful like poor Miss Lacy, or even bitter like Mrs. Pritchett.

The housekeeper came herself to summon her to Mr. Glendower. Her eyes were sharp with malice which tinged her voice. "The master is in the breakfast room. He has been informed by Mrs. Mowbray of your conduct last night." She showed clearly her vengeful anticipation of Miranda's imminent dismissal.

Mr. Glendower leaned back in his chair, the remains of his breakfast still on the table, a steaming cup of coffee before him.

Miranda paused inside the doorway, and Mrs. Pritchett gave her a push. "Go on in then. Mr. Glendower has work to do. He can't sit around for you."

She followed Miranda to the table, and the two women waited while Mr. Glendower took a sip of coffee, keeping his eyes on Miranda. There was speculation in their dark depths, but his expression did not reveal his thoughts. The housekeeper stood with hands folded over her stomach, and Mr. Glendower said, "There is no need to remain, Mrs. Pritchett, but be so good as to stay within call."

Her face darkened with anger as she turned and stalked out, not quite daring to bang the door behind her.

"Sit down, Miranda."

She stayed quite still. "If you have something unpleasant to say then I wish you will get it over quickly. I cannot bear any more."

The last words burst out of her involuntarily, and her eyes filled with tears which she dashed away with her hand.

Mr. Glendower's strong fingers tapped the table, then he repeated forcefully, "Sit down, Miranda."

This time she obeyed, and he said evenly, "Certain complaints have been brought to my attention. In the general way I do not make the intrigues of my servants my affair, and I turn a blind eye to their love tangles provided they are not obtrusive and do not interfere with the comfort of my household, but your case, I feel, is different.

"My wife, you see, has this notion of promoting you to be some sort of companion to Miss Angharad and Miss Mowbray. You might be a good deal in their company. I am told that your skill in sewing is remarkable, but my wife is given to exaggeration so you may be indifferent for all I know."

Or for all you care, thought Miranda. She sat with hands folded loosely in her lap, watching her employer as he paused to stare out of the window. She shrink in inward shame as she remembered his arms about her in last night's storm and the feel of his lips on hers. Was he also remembering? Did he, too, know self-disgust at his temporary lapse? He spoke abruptly. "You told me that you found Merrick odious. I cannot reconcile your statement with the knowledge that you were discovered with him in an —immodest position."

"I was drenched when I returned from my walk. I needed to wring out my gown. I needed warmth from the kitchen fire. Mr. Merrick heard me and found me there, but I had my cloak about me. He . . . he misunderstood my situation. Mrs. Pritchett arrived. I little thought I should feel gratitude to her."

Mr. Glendower's eyes searched her face. "Could you not have waited until you reached the security of your room before disrobing? You are mature enough to realise that your action placed you in a most ambiguous condition."

Miranda leapt to her feet. "Yes, I was unwise, but my . . . my room, you say! A garret which my Papa would have considered fit only for storage. And I am to share it with two others, and only through the kindness of a poor mistreated little kitchen skivvy am I able to have a bed of my own, if you can call it that!

"I did not expect luxury when I hired myself out as a domestic, but any human being should expect comfort at least as great as you give your horses. My brief glimpses of your stables lead me to believe I would prefer to share their quarters than to exist in my present state."

His astonished look turned to anger, and she felt a stab of fear and turned to hurry away, but he was after her, overturning a chair in his haste. He caught her arm and pulled her to face him. "That is the second time you have accused me of neglecting my dependents. I employ, at damnable expense, an army of servants in this travesty of a home, and the money I allocate is excessively generous, yet you find fault. Why?"

Miranda struggled to escape. "I refuse to answer you. You believe me capable of base conduct with a man I despise. I want only to pack and leave here."

He caught her other arm, and for an instant she was held so close that she could feel the vibrations of his heartbeats. She remained motionless, her eyes imploring mercy, even while she knew a treacherous wish to stay near him. Then he said gently, "Tempestuous child, you are well named. Please, Miranda, do me the favour of talking with me. Sit and I will pour coffee for you, and we will discuss your position here. Do you take cream? Sugar?"

She might have been an honoured guest as she replied, "Cream only, please."

He laughed.

"How many suitors have told you, when you refuse sugar, that you are sweet enough?"

She smiled tremulously. "One or two," she confessed.

"As I suspected. I wonder that you have not married, especially when you were left so ill-provided with the means to live."

"My Papa was too generous to leave much! It was only his goodness which prevented . . ."

He raised a protesting hand. "Spare me, I beg of you. I accept all that you say of your father. I simply asked why you had not thought fit to marry."

Stifling a desire to tell him to mind his own business she said, "I have never cared sufficiently for anyone to wish to enter into a relationship which . . ."

She caught the sardonic gleam in his eyes and paused,

flushing. "I am not obliged to tell you, sir."

"Indeed you are not, Miranda. I am amazed at your forbearance towards me. Tell me, though, do you desire to remain in my employ? You seem to have made an unfortunate beginning."

When she hesitated, he continued. "I would have expected a girl of your quick temperament always to have a ready answer. You are intelligent, educated, and must sense the unhappy strife which rules here. Now I must stay because Ynys Noddfa has always been my home and will be so until I die. But you can go. I will give you the return fare to London, first class naturally, and a little extra for your convenience and write you a glowing reference. What say you to that?"

Their glances met, and she surprised something in his which she could not fathom. She would have said that he was anxious over her reply, but that must be impossible. He frowned. "Come now, Miranda, you must decide. And while talking of journeys, I will say now that I sent my cousin adequate travel allowance to cover any expenses. Mrs. Mowbray meant no harm by her parsimony, even if she did try to conceal it from me by having you change compartments at the last lap. She has had to become used to watching the pennies. Her husband died, leaving her poor, and she must make economies. In your case I feel she was wrong."

He gave a short laugh. "And do you know what she purchased with part of the money she saved? A revolving bed table for my wife. A new-fangled horror which will encourage her to spend even more time reclining in bed."

"Please, Mr. Glendower, I cannot endure hearing you talk so of your wife. Especially to me."

"Especially to you? Now why is that?"

"Because . . . because I am only a servant here. Is is not fitting."

"Servant be damned! You could never be that if you spent the rest of your life attempting it. For all your brave tries at downcast eyes and a humble response, you sound exactly what you are."

Miranda's colour rose. "I did not know. I had not intended to be disrespectful. Perhaps Mrs. Pritchett has some grounds for her dislike of me. Well, I will try to do better . . ."

"Then you will stay. Splendid, Miranda. It is just what I hoped. This household stands sorely in need of your refreshing honesty."

He jumped up and walked to the door, and Miranda lowered the hand she had raised in a half-hearted protest. She did not want to go. She knew that in her heart. So she would stay, and attempt to come to terms with her new life. And she left unheeded the inner warning which suggested that she should examine her motives more closely.

Mr. Glendower opened the breakfast-room door. "Mrs. Pritchett, will you come in, please."

The housekeeper entered, an anticipatory smile on her thin lips. "Is she ready to . . .?"

Her jaw dropped at the sight of Miranda, seated at the table, her coffee in the translucent bone-china cup untouched.

Mr. Glendower gestured towards Miranda. "Mrs. Pritchett, there seem to have been misunderstandings surrounding Miss Courtney. In the bustle of arrival and settling in, Mrs. Mowbray quite forgot to inform you that she was engaged partly as a companion to the young ladies. True, she will be undertaking some fine sewing and teaching, but in future she will be living in a style more suited to her status. I would be obliged if you would have a room prepared for her and instruct the other servants that she will be addressed in a formal manner by them. Thank you, Mrs. Pritchett. That is all."

The housekeeper's mouth closed, and she swallowed with difficulty. Her face was dark with suspicion as she looked from Miranda to her master, and the look she gave Miranda before departing was venomous.

"Such an unpleasant woman," said Mr. Glendower. "I cannot think how my wife came to engage her. I suppose, though, she is all smiles when it suits her.

"Now, Miranda, I think it is time you took over duties more fitted to your—temperament."

A footman came in answer to the bell, and all his

71

training could not prevent a fleeting expression of astonishment as his employer ordered. "Conduct Miss Courtney to the school room, Thomas. She will be in charge there in future. In fact, we had better assign a maid to keep the place orderly. What was the name of the skivvy, Miranda?"

"Gwennie. Oh, do you really mean to allow her to leave the kitchen? Oh, sir, that is good of you." Her deep blue eyes shone with gratitude, and her cheeks were delicately flushed. She turned to the footman. "Tell Gwennie, if you please, that I will see her at once. Tell her to come as she is. I will attend to any problems she has concerning dress."

Mr. Glendower gave a shout of laughter. "You a servant! It's a good thing I rescued you. Mrs. Pritchett would have destroyed you!"

"Don't say that—even in fun."

He took her hand to help her to rise to her feet and said too softly for the footman's ears. "Why I do believe you are truly afraid of her. What nonsense! In any case, you are out of her power now. Go with Thomas and make what you like of the schoolroom. It is quite a comfortable place."

He was right, and Miranda drew a long breath of pleasure as she looked at it. The room was long, and its several latticed windows faced east, overlooking the estuary. We shall have the morning sun, she thought happily. The floor was of highly polished oak, with bright rugs, and at one end was a fireplace before which was a deep piled carpet and easy chairs. The customary desks and stools were near the windows, and Miranda pictured herself here with the two young ladies. They could sew and talk and be altogether cosy. The door opened and Gwennie entered, her mouth round with astonishment.

"Matilda, it's true is it then? Mrs. Pritchett is in such a fury as no one has ever seen her before. When I got your message I could hardly believe my ears. And Mrs. Pritchett said . . ." She stopped abruptly, and her face reddened beneath the kitchen grime.

"Yes, Gwennie, what did Mrs. Pritchett say?"

"A lot of nonsense, which I for one don't credit. And I'd rather not repeat it."

"I wish you to do so. I do not trust that woman. She seems determined to be my enemy, and I must know how to protect myself. How can I do so if my friends, and I hope I count you one, do not help me?"

"Oh, am I your friend? I never was such a thing before. When you don't know your Mam and Dad and come from a poorhouse, no one cares to have you for a friend. Even Myfanwy looks down on me. She comes from the village, see, and her Mam and Dad wanted her."

Miranda bent forward to take the rough little hand in hers. "You are still a child, yet you have known so much unhappiness. I will do my best to make life happier for you, but please do as I ask. In general I would not interest myself in gossip, but I feel I should know what Mrs. Pritchett is saying. Will you not tell me?"

Gwennie, still holding Miranda's hand, said hesitantly, "It's not so much what she said—it's the way she spoke. Well—she said that you and the master were on *very* friendly terms when she was called back to the breakfast parlour and that a room is to be made up for you. And then you'll be sleeping alone, and what with Mrs. Glendower being so sickly and them not hitting it off so well . . . she stopped there, Matilda, but it was enough to make the others snigger and . . . and . . . oh, Matilda, I don't believe a word of it. You're so good!"

Miranda went rigid with anger, but she patted Gwennie's hand before relinquishing it and walking to the window. The previous night's high tide had refilled the pools and channels, but now the sky was blue and the wind had dried the sand and was raising miniature sand storms, which rose and settled in the innocent-looking sea grasses, which could prove a trap for the unwary.

All thought was driven away when the door burst open with a crash and Angharad almost leapt into the room. "You snake-in-the-grass! You viper! You lied to me! I knew it was only a ruse to make me accept another prissy governess. Seamstress indeed! You must think me gullible indeed."

Miranda glanced at Gwennie, who again showed so

much amazement that Miranda felt a wild desire to laugh. If her own life was being upended, how much more so was Gwennie's, thrust into the world upstairs from her sordid, but familiar existence below. "Gwennie," she said kindly, "I wish you will go to the kitchen and procure a supply of dusters, mops and polishes. Then I will find material to make you a suitable dress. Later I will speak to Mrs. Glendower about your garments. Yours are inadequate for upstairs duties."

As the maid scuttled away, Miranda faced Angharad calmly. "In future, my child, I must ask you not to create scenes before the servants. I must ask you also to remember that I do not lie. Not only am I *not* your governess, but I am ill-qualified to be anybody's.

"I could instruct you in reading and history perhaps, but as for mathematics I am woefully stupid. My accomplishments lie in my hands, and if you would care to learn some of my skills I will be delighted to impart them to you. I gather that I shall be doing some plain sewing as well, so I expect I shall spend only part of my time with you, though I intend to equire if I must ever return to that nasty little sewing room again. I much prefer it here.

"I can assure you, Angharad, that I was engaged as a seamstress, and it is your own Mama who wishes me to be a companion to you."

"I will vouch for that," said a gentle voice, and Ellen Mowbray entered the room. "Is my cousin being difficult, Miranda? Mama said she probably would be. She seems to be a most undisciplined child."

"How dare you criticize me, Ellen! I wish Mr. Glendower had never sent for you and your odious mother. We were perfectly happy. Now there seems nowhere I can escape from censure unless it be over the dunes."

She turned to leave, her green eyes flashing emerald through the tangle of untended titian hair, which tumbled over her forehead, and Miranda caught her arm.

"Please don't go, Angharad. I do so understand how irritating it is when you never get a moment to yourself. I was the youngest of a large family, and my brothers were such teases and my sisters often so stern."

As her words penetrated the child stopped struggling. One hand swept aside the knotted hair, and the scowl turned to a reluctant smile. "I have been impolite to you."

Miranda stayed quite still. The child seemed to behave so abruptly that it was impossible to know how best to act until they were better acquainted. This time it seemed she had done the right thing.

"You are no governess," declared Angharad. "By now a governess would have been quoting long Bible passages at me about humility and obedience. Did you really get into mischief when you were little? Will you tell me of your brothers and sisters? I have so longed for someone else in the family, but there will be no one now. My Mama will never . . ."

"Be silent!" Ellen's voice rapped, and both girls stared at her. Her usually colourless face was suffused with pink, and her pale eyes shone. "It is not fitting that you should speak so of your parents, Cousin Angharad. Sometimes you seem to possess knowledge quite beyond what is proper for your years, but you are not old enough to comprehend the true meaning of love between husband and wife. Your Papa's first concern is to protect your Mama, whose health is so wretched."

Angharad laughed harshly. "What do you know, little goody two shoes? Have you ever been married? No, you haven't, and you have never even had a suitor, have you? And not likely to from what I see. Isn't that why your mother brought you here?"

The colour died from Ellen's face as she stared at her cousin. "Why . . . why what can you mean?"

"Nothing. I meant nothing." Angharad's full lips were compressed and she looked sulky.

But you cannot have made such a statement without purport. How can my being here have any lasting effect upon my . . . my . . .

"Lack of lovers?" finished Angharad. The sulky look had been replaced by one of malicious amusement.

Miranda saw, to her concern, that tears were welling into the pale blue eyes and trickling on to Ellen's cheeks. She felt sympathy mixed with exasperation. If a cousin of hers had spoken so to her, she would probably have boxed her ears and shaken the meaning out of her, but it was useless to expect such tactics from Ellen. She felt puzzled. Her own ambiguous position in the household made her uncertain how to proceed. Clearly Angharad had caught some half-truth and twisted it into a confused meaning.

"Angharad," said Miranda softly, "you have wounded your cousin with your heedless remarks. Do, please, explain yourself; or else apologise for your rudeness."

"Apologise? That I will not! And before you have been long in this house, Miss Miranda Courtney, you will discover that dear Cousin Augusta believes my Mama to be in a decline and that she has brought her unmarriageable daughter here in an effort to gain her the affections of Mr. Glendower. But he will not look at her. He will not care for her lack-lustre ways. He will not, I say!

"And as for you, miss seamstress, you may learn to keep your place and not to interfere in matters which are not your concern."

Miranda gasped, not at Angharad's insolence to her, but at the shocking implication of her insinuations about Ellen. She stole a glance at Ellen, whose face was now paper white. She swayed a little, and Miranda made to go to her, but before she could do so there was a swift step from the door behind her, and Mr. Glendower had reached the half-fainting girl.

He supported her to a chair then turned to Angharad. "Be so kind as to fetch a restorative. Probably your mother's room would be the best place to try—she has every remedy there, God knows."

His daughter did not move, but stared at her father as he massaged Ellen's hands, and her eyes glowed green.

"Obey me," he ordered, and she raced away.

She was soon back, panting for breath, and Miranda held the smelling salts beneath Ellen's nose. She gasped, and a little colour returned to her cheeks, and Mr. Glendower rose. Miranda wondered how much of their conversation he might have overheard.

He spoke gravely to his daughter. "I came to see if Miranda had found things to her liking here. I was astonished as I approached to hear you shouting like a fish-wife. You will be good enough to explain to me."

Miranda waited for the unpredictable girl to lash herself once more into a fury, but Angharad stood quietly, her hands writhing together, her eyes fixed on her father in a mute plea of such piteous anguish that Miranda stepped involuntarily towards her.

Mr. Glendower waved her back. "You will answer me, Angharad. I heard your insolence towards Miranda. I will not have such unseemly speech beneath my roof. How did this situation arise?"

There was a small strangled cry from Ellen, who then said, "Pray Cousin Gethin, do not pursue the matter. A . . . a storm in a teacup I do assure you." She gave a ghastly smile, and Miranda ached with sympathy, remembering Angharad's accusation, and longed to add her appeal to Ellen's for him to forget his anger. But he seemed far more displeased than the situation warranted. Children were often rude and disobedient, and Anharad looked remorseful.

She stepped close to her father. "Please do not look at me so," she begged. "I cannot endure it. I would not hurt you for all the world."

She tried to take his hand, but he drew back, and the child flinched and looked stricken. Miranda felt a wild anger within her. How could a father treat his child so cruelly? And how could he expect rational behaviour from her when all she seemed to have had was a mother who spent her life in bed, a houseful of servants ruled by a despot, and a father who seemingly disliked her touch?

Mr. Glendower stared round at the three girls. "It seems that there is a conspiracy of silence. You, Cousin Ellen, and Miranda, will not help this unruly child by condoning her disorderly humours. I must hope that your reasoning powers prevail and that between you, you may be able to instal more amiable qualities in her."

After he had left there was a short silence, and the memory of Angharad's accusation returned to Miranda in force, as it did to Ellen, who rose and said shakily, "Angharad, your father is right in condemning you even though he did not know the extent of your wickedness.

77

For it is wicked of you to say such bad things about my mother and me. But I will not allow a moment's thoughtlessness to come between us. I would like to be your friend —if you will allow me."

Miranda esteemed such magnanimity and strength of purpose, but Angharad laughed harshly. "You and I can never be friends, Ellen. Go to your Mama if you do not believe me, and ask her why she has come now when she has never before offered help."

Ellen spoke through white lips. "My own Papa needed us. Now he is . . . gone . . . Mama is free. And it is the first time your Papa has asked for assistance. We were told that Cousin Lora's illness has advanced alarmingly."

"One wonders if dear Cousin Augusta would have been so quick to answer his call if her dear daughter had not *advanced* so far towards spinsterhood.

"And in any case they say that Mama's sickness has grown worse only in her mind. That is what I have heard. And you will find that Mr. Glendower will not be tempted by such . . . such insipid fare as you, Ellen."

She ran from the room, leaving the door swinging, and both girls listened to the sound of her retreating footsteps. Miranda could hardly bear the look of humiliation on Ellen's face. She was too vulnerable, and Miranda felt concern for her in this turbulent household. She was like a fragile plant, wrongly transposed to a jungle, and Miranda watched her walk silently to the door and made no attempt to speak. She could think of no words to use.

Chapter Six

Yet in spite of the disquieting emotions which seemed to fill Ynys Noddfa, Miranda found a measure of contentment as she helped Gwennie to clean the dusty schoolroom, gaining pleasure in performing the homely tasks she had used to do with Mama.

And when Thomas told her that her new bedroom was prepared, she was filled with delighted relief. It was in the old part of the house and overlooking the sea, but on a lower floor and so different from the attic. She leaned her back on the thick oak door and stared about her. The room was as plain as Mrs. Glendower's was cluttered, but it held the gracious simplicity of an earlier age with its walls of red silk and carved wooden panels. And there was no jumbled confusion of pictures. The largest was an ordered Dutch landscape. On the opposite wall a splash of colour became, when she examined it more closely, a painting of a sailing boat in the setting sun. It was signed Claude Monet, and she liked the deep pinks and golds which seemed to shimmer with light, though the name meant nothing to her. The third was a water colour, clearly painted by an amateur hand, but pleasing, and Miranda realised that it showed Ynys Noddfa many years ago, before the Victorian wing had been added. Previous Glendowers had evidently employed architects of discernment, and she could assume only that when Gethin Glendower had permitted the addition of the new rather vulgar-looking wing, he had been trying blindly to please his new bride.

The carpet was of a modern oriental design, its patterned square leaving the surrounding areas of polished wood visible, but someone had chosen it with care for its colours blended perfectly with the red and gold satin of the bedhangings and quilt.

Miranda laughed to herself. A four-poster bed! She walked to it and sat down. The bed might be old, but care had been taken that she would sleep softly on feathers.

Her luggage had been left near a mahogany chest-of-drawers, and she took pleasure in folding her clothes neatly away and hanging her few gowns in the new wardrobe, which had also been chosen to blend with the other furnishings.

When she had finished, she poured water from the cream-coloured ewer into the bowl, which stood on the pretty Regency washstand, and splashed her face and hands, and when she reached out automatically for a towel her fingers found one which was soft and snowy white.

Then she brushed her hair and tied it back and surveyed herself in the cheval glass. Her plain drab gown could not conceal the graceful curves of her body, or hide her beauty, which was increased by pink cheeks and eyes glowing with health and the excitement engendered by this turn of events.

Someone knocked and when she called, there was Gwennie, who now seemed to have a perpetual look of astonishment.

"Miss Courtney," she breathed, "Mr. Glendower says that is your proper name and we must all call you by it, do you know that this is a guest room? Mrs. Pritchett had got another attic ready, so she had, but the master said that he and the mistress wanted you in a nice room. Oh, Matilda—" her hand flew to her mouth—"I mean, Miss Courtney, isn't it all wonderful!"

"Wonderful," agreed Miranda.

"But miss, if you could see Mr. Merrick and 'specially Mrs. Pritchett . . .!"

Miranda shuddered. "Thank you, but I have no desire to do so." As Gwennie continued to gape around her, Miranda enquired gently, "Did you come here for a specific purpose, Gwennie?"

Again the little hand was clapped over her mouth.

"Oh, miss, I forgot. I was that excited, you see. Yes indeed, Mrs. Mowbray wants you to meet her and the young ladies in the schoolrom in ten minutes and bring your sewing things and some examples of your work, 'specially the lace."

"Thank you, Gwennie. You may help me gather things together, that is, if you have no other orders for anyone."

"Oh, no, miss, I'm to do what you say now. Those are to be my only tasks, Mr. Glendower says. Oh, miss, I don't think I've ever been so happy."

Miranda and Gwennie waited for a few minutes for the arrival of the others at the schoolroom. Angharad was clearly reluctant and pulling against the grasp held on her arm by Mrs. Mowbray, who announced, "We will sit by the window. Gwennie and Matilda—Miranda I should say—you can carry that table over here. It does not look to be heavy. Then you, Miranda, be so good as to set out some sewing of yours for the girls to examine. Miss Ellen is a fair hand with her needle, but I desire her to become proficient in the art of making needlepoint lace. You will teach her."

Miranda felt doubtful. "I will try, Mrs. Mowbray, but I feel I must say that I was instructed from a very early age and have had much practice under the guidance of an expert. It is not an accomplishment to be acquired swiftly. It is not easy. Would it not be better perhaps to begin with something simpler?"

Mrs. Mowbray raised her lorgnette from her quivering bosom. "Are you intending to imply that my daughter could not be as skilful as yourself?"

"Oh, no, indeed not. Eventually perhaps—it is just that —well, we will try. We can certainly do that."

"I wish to learn also," demanded Argharad.

Miranda looked at the girl, whose hair was imperfectly brushed and whose expensive frock and kid shoes were unkempt and dishevelled. "It requires a high degree of neatness to perform anything so fine."

Angharad set her mouth in mutinuous lines and glared back at Miranda before she said loudly, "You are still a servant here, remember, for all your airs and graces. You must do as I want."

"That will do, Angharad," said Mrs. Mowbray, but the mildness of her tone indicated that she shared the girl's sentiments. Some of Miranda's exultation drained away. True, she had been given a pretty apartment and was to be a companion of sorts to the young ladies of the house, but she must remind herself that she was still employed here in a humble capacity and subject to the whims even of Angharad, the daughter of the house.

"Miss Angharad," she answered mildly, "I will endeavour to teach you anything you wish, but truly it would be more practical if both you and Miss Ellen were to attempt some easier thing to begin with." She turned to Mrs. Mowbray. "I will guide them to master the very fine stitching which will be required before we begin the actual learning."

Mrs. Mowbray snorted. "Show *me* what has to be done, and I will be the one to come to a decision."

Miranda opened her workbox and took out a collar she had begun in Walter's house, together with the fine cotton threads and needles. "You must begin," she explained, "by drawing your design on paper and lining it with parchment. Fortunately I have this piece of work already by me. The thing to remember is that however complicated the design, it is always achieved by using single looped stitches, often only of the buttonhole variety. I think that patience and delicacy are the virtues one needs in this sort of lace making."

She studied her pattern to remind herself of its intricacies, and Mrs. Mowbray began to tap her foot and Angharad to sigh with impatience, though Ellen remained still, her hands meekly folded on her lap.

"I am sorry for the delay," said Miranda, "but the work is finely detailed and requires a good deal of concentration—at least until the pattern is mastered. This collar is a mixture of Venetian and Brussels lace, which are distinguished by the difference in the arrangement of stitches . . ."

"Begin to sew," interrupted Angharad. "We shall learn more than by listening."

Miranda's needle began to dart in and out of the braid edging. Knowing that only one of the watchers was at

they were silent for a moment, listening to the rustle of her dress as she stalked along the corridor.

Gwennie crept out from behind a cupboard, her hand over her mouth, her eyes enormous, and Angharad turned on her. "Have you been there all the while, you little spy? What are you hoping to find out, eh? Who told you to listen?"

She had seized Gwennie's arm in a tight grip and gave her a shake with each question.

Gwennie was clearly terrified. "N . . . nothing, Miss Angharad, I'm not spying. I was reaching to polish a patch of dust I missed when you all started . . . started . . ." She stopped and gazed appealingly into her tormentor's face. "I meant no harm, miss."

"Let her go!" Miranda's authoritative voice caused Angharad to stop molesting Gwennie before she realised who had spoken, then her quick temper flared again.

"Who are you to give orders to me? You are only . . ."

"Remember your father's caution," reminded Ellen, and Angharad stopped speaking, her face contorted in suppressed fury and tears rained down her cheeks.

Miranda regarded her with puzzled exasperation. The girl behaved like a wayward baby. What was to be done with her? Scarcely daring to hope that it would prove a distraction, she ventured, "Would you like to see my sampler, Angharad? It is in my room."

Instantly the tears stopped, and Angharad's full lips stretched in a smile of great sweetness. "Oh, yes, I would. Now! At once!"

"I will fetch it. No, Gwennie, I think you may not be able to find it. I have put it away beneath some . . . some other things."

She knew perfectly well that the sampler was under the blue-green brocade and shimmering silver-grey silk and wanted no excited comments from the maid to draw attention to her pretensions to finery.

But Angharad said immediately, "I will accompany you, Miranda. I should like to see your new room."

"In that case," said Ellen, rising, "I may as well come, too. It will save you an unnecessary journey."

Miranda sighed. She could think of no reasonable

excuse for refusing their company, yet the thought of this invasion of her privacy irritated her. She felt that there should be one place in her life where her seclusion should be inviolable, but she supposed she must learn to accept that, having left the protection of her family and taken on this position, she had relinquished the privileges granted a lady of birth.

Seeing the eager look on Gwennie's face she smiled. "Since my humble childish efforts seem to have instigated an expedition, you had better join us."

Gwennie grinned and followed the short procession. She often found it difficult to follow Miss Courtney's high-flown English, but her starved heart reacted instinctively to kindness.

Angharad looked around Miranda's bedroom. "Mr. Glendower has certainly seen that you will sleep in comfort, Miranda. Did you know that he gave orders personally for the preparation? The room was protected by holland covers. We never have visitors now. Well . . ." her eyes flickered over Ellen ". . . almost never, and you are not exactly a visitor, are you cousin. Visitors are people who stay for pleasure and enjoyment, and Cousin Augusta had purpose in bringing you here . . ."

Miranda and Ellen stared at Angharad, who laughed and darted to the window. "Oh, you have a good view of the sea! How calm it is today. Yet it can be so turbulent at times. Just like people, eh, Miranda? You like storms, don't you?"

It was evident that she had heard about Miranda's escapade. What had she deduced from the gossip she seemed to garner so readily? Miranda shivered. This lovely child seemed so odd a mixture of infantile behaviour and worldly knowledge. What damage she could do if she tried.

Ellen spoke quietly. "The sampler, Miranda."

Miranda flushed. "I beg your pardon, Miss Ellen, I was lost in thought. It is in here."

She attempted to open the drawer and extract the sampler before Angharad left the window, but almost as if sensing her urgency, the child was across the room in one of her darting movements, and her sharp green eyes instantly caught what Miranda was trying to hide.

"Miranda! What is it? Those lovely materials! Oh, do let me see them, please do."

"They are simply waiting an opportunity for me to make them into a gown," said Miranda coolly, "and that, I think, will not be for some time, as I shall have no cause to wear anything so fine while I am here."

Angharad pulled at the blue-green brocade and rubbed it rapturously against her cheek. "Oh, it's so silky, so pretty. You must make a gown quickly. Mama's birthday falls in October, and we always have a party then. She followed the custom when she came here as a bride, and it is expected. I think it will have to be held because otherwise people will think it so curious. It is a tradition, you see. Mr. Glendower will not want a tradition broken."

Miranda's control was shaken. "Angharad, I wish you would not be so precipitate. You have no right to grab things from my private drawer without asking. And why do you constantly refer to your Papa as 'Mr. Glendower'? It is neither seemly, nor loving, for a daughter to speak so when she is among family."

"But you are not family!"

"You are being foolish and petty."

"What do you know about it? What do any of you know? I have learned of matters which would amaze you if I told you, but I won't! We have secrets in this house that you outsiders will never discover. At least, not until . . . until . . . well, never mind, I have said enough."

"In my view, Cousin Angharad, you have said too much, but shall we forget it just now? Miranda was kind enough to allow us into her room, and we should not abuse her hospitality. Shall we see the sampler now?"

Miranda felt a sudden warmth towards Ellen. There was more to her than one could comprehend on first acquaintance. She looked at her now as she bent her pale head over the sampler. In her beige gown with braids of fawn she looked dull. Why could she not dress in more becoming colours? She might even be pretty with the right clothes and more animation, but she *was* kind and that seemed a quality much lacking in Ynys Noddfa.

Angharad took the sampler and laid it on the quilt, where it looked, to Miranda, with its small embroidered house with the improbably large birds on the roof, the formalised trees and pattern of leaves round the border, a pathetic and sad reminder of her happy, lost life.

"This is the alphabet," pronounced Angharad. She peered closely and began to trace the words at the bottom with her forefinger. "Pl . . . pleas . . . ant words are as a . . . a hon . . . ey . . . honey . . . What is that last word, Miranda?"

"Honeycomb," supplied Miranda, hiding her amazement at the girl's inability to decipher the words. At the age of twelve, which was what she judged Angharad to be, she herself had enjoyed reading Papa's books and copying out his sermons.

"Pleasant words are as a honeycomb," repeated Ellen. "What a good saying that is. 'Sweet to the soul and kind to the bones,'" she finished the proverb.

Miranda smiled at her. "You know your Bible, Miss Ellen."

Ellen returned the smile. "It is a sentiment that my cousin would do well to remember. Kind words are not costly, Angharad, and mean much to others."

Angharad had picked up the sampler to examine the stitches, but now she tossed it onto the bed. "Preaching! Preaching! That's all I ever get. I refuse to make a sampler if I have to put some stupid words like those on it."

She darted from the room, slamming the door, and Ellen bit her lip. "I should not have provoked her. I forget sometimes how intolerant she is. I had better go after her and make my peace."

Left alone with Gwennie, Miranda was about to return the sampler to the drawer when the little maid said, "Could I have a look, please, miss. I never saw one of those before."

"Of course, my dear. Forgive me, I was not thinking."

"Pleasant words are as a honeycomb," mused Gwennie. "That's lovely, miss. Did you choose it yourself?"

"Yes, as a matter of fact I did. But I did not know you could read English, Gwennie."

"Oh, miss, I can't. I can't even read my own language.

No one ever managed to teach me see. But I remember things I've heard. Is your name here?"

"Yes, right at the bottom. Here it is—Miranda Hamilton Courtney, aged thirteen years, 1870."

Gwennie's rough finger touched the name gently. "Miranda," she said, then again, "Miranda. I'll know your name, miss. I'll never forget it."

Miranda smiled before saying that they must return to the schoolroom. The others were not there so she stitched quietly at the collar while Gwennie tidied. The door opened and Ellen entered looking pink and cross. "That child is impossible! I apologised for what I said, though really I do not think it was so bad, and it is nothing but the truth anyway, but she bade me leave her in most unladylike terms. Evidently she has mixed too much with servants and grooms."

Miranda half rose, but Ellen shook her head. "It is of no use to look for her because she has left the house. She said she was going to walk in the dunes. She bade me tell you that she will collect grasses."

Ellen stood staring out over the estuary. "The tide is coming in. This seems so odd a place to me, Miranda. For much of the time we are prisoners here. At least, that is how I feel." She shivered. "I wish Mama had not come. Do you feel no sense of oppression, Miranda?"

"It . . . it is very beautiful on the island. Yet I understand you. Ynys Noddfa is not . . . not a comfortable home. There seems to be so restless a spirit here."

"I knew you felt it, too. And I cannot tell when we shall return to London. We are very poor now, and when Angharad said that I had never had a suitor, she was telling the truth. Well, there was once a music master whom Mama would not even consider. I did not care for him, I confess, but I found his attentions flattering.

"Papa could have given me an attractive dowry had he not lost all his money before he passed away. Mama says that men will marry plain women only when they have money."

Miranda made a gesture of protest, but Ellen laughed and said briskly, "I do not know what I am about, Miranda. Here are you, a girl of birth, having to earn

89

your living because you are too high principled to marry where you do not love, and I burden you with my nonsense. Will you come to my room, please, and measure me for my gowns?"

Ellen's room in the new wing was as neat and prosaic as her person. On her chest-of-drawers lay a pair of silver-backed brushes, an ivory comb and a bottle of lavendar water. By her bed was a copy of the Bible and a book entitled *Daily Steps Towards Heaven*.

"My Mama does not permit novels." Ellen's voice was dry, and Miranda flushed. She had been staring round showing quite clearly her surprise at the bareness of the room.

"Many mothers feel the same," she stammered. "I'm sure I do not . . ."

"Pray don't continue, my dear. I do not confine my reading to religious tomes, I assure you. One of my consolations is to pore over the romances of others. I'm afraid I deceive poor Mama a little, but I could not stand life without some diversion."

She opened the bottom drawer of her chest-of-drawers and removed a stack of plain under-garments to reveal several novels. Chuckling a little, she closed the drawer. "At one time I never would have behaved in so clandestine a fashion, but I am a woman now and cannot permit Mama to dictate absolutely to me."

Then from another drawer she drew a quantity of materials. They were different in texture, but all equally tedious in shade. Buff, beige, tan and a watered poplin of ochre. Ellen pointed to the latter. "That is to be my party frock," she explained. "If my cousins do give a reception for Cousin Lora's birthday, I assume I shall need it. Charming, is it not?"

Miranda opened and closed her mouth, and Ellen laughed, startling Miranda with the sound of genuine amusement. "My dear girl," continued Ellen, "you have an expressive face. I saw at once what you thought of my garb when we met."

"Oh, Miss Ellen, I am so sorry. I did not mean to hurt you."

"You did not. I liked you for your honesty and was

glad when Mama chose you to accompany us."

She tossed the materials onto the bed. "Mama says that one can always pick out a lady by the inconspicuous colours and designs of her attire. Am not I the perfect lady, Miranda? Will not you enjoy helping me to make up these delightful shades into equally delicious gowns?"

"Miss Ellen, I . . ."

"Miranda, spare me. While we are alone, let me be plain 'Ellen.' I would welcome your friendship."

Miranda smiled her assent, gratified by Ellen's confidence. Clearly there was a good deal more animation than she had suspected hidden beneath the girl's pliable demeanour. Ellen laughed suddenly. "I was so delighted when I found you had hidden those lovely materials away. It gave me courage to come to a resolve."

Again she opened the bottom drawer and from the back she drew a length of dark-blue shining Damassin. Miranda gasped with pleasure as Ellen, with a deft gesture, allowed the damask to unfold to a gleaming fall, which she held against her body. The silver flowers woven into the fabric caught the silvery gold of Ellen's hair, the colour deepened her eyes, and the dark shade emphasized the delicacy of her complexion, which was rosy now with excitement.

"Ellen! You look so pretty! But your Mama will never allow it to be made up."

"She will not know. I am going to beg your help as I am a poor needlewoman, but I will take full responsibility. I will say, if necessary, that you believed this to be my Mama's choice. I had to save my pin money for months and evade Mama in Swan and Edgar's to buy the material, and I will not be thwarted now. Please help me."

Miranda agreed. Mrs. Mowbray would be angry she did not doubt, but she so sympathized with Ellen that she felt she could brave her mother's wrath.

The Damassin once more hidden, the two girls decided to try to find Angharad. The cool breeze of the past few days had dropped, and the sun shone so warmly that they were able to go out without cloaks. Ellen carried a parasol, and Miranda pulled on a pretty chip-straw hat with pink flowers and ribbons, ignoring the fact that brims were unfashionable. Rain on her face was one thing; a nose peeled by the sun something quite different.

They were about to leave the house when Gethin Glendower entered the hall and looked about him. "Where is Angharad? Does she not accompany you on your walk?"

Ellen said, "My cousin went ahead of us. We are going to join her."

His dark eyes searched their faces. "What you mean, I suppose, is that she has flown out in one of her tantrums, and you must waste time searching for her. I will join you. I shall have something to say to that young miss."

The tide was almost full, and as they walked along the boulder-strewn sand Gethin Glendower took the path nearest the sea and seemed careless of the occasional wave which touched his boots. He wore his tweeds, and Miranda now realised that they were like comfortable and comforting friends, just as Papa's old velvet jacket had been to him, and she found the idea touching. She had learned from Gwennie's chatter that he was wealthy, having an income from properties in London and the north, from farms in other parts of Wales and from a slate mine in the nearby hills.

The beach curved inwards, and they rounded a storm-sculptured rock which jutted from the cliff, to see Angharad standing on a boulder around which the tide swirled as she gazed out to sea.

She seemed to sense their presence and turned. For a moment she stared before leaping across the stretch of water which divided her from the shore. A wave caught and soaked her to the knees, but they saw her laugh as she ran to them, sliding and stumbling among the pebbles.

"Angharad! Be careful!" called Gethin, but he was too late. She was keeping her eyes fixed on her father and tripped, failed to regain her balance and fell. She made an attempt to rise, fell again and lay still.

Gethin reached her first, and when the two girls arrived he was kneeling with Angharad's head pillowed on his left arm as he patted her hands and face. His face was inexpressibly concerned as he said. "Angharad, my little one. Angharad! Pray God she is not badly hurt."

He smoothed the rich auburn hair from Angharad's white forehead, revealing an ugly bruise, and put his ear close to her mouth. "Her breathing is even. I think she is only stunned. Miranda, dampen this handkerchief. Ellen, pull off her wet boots and chafe her feet."

Moments later, Angharad's long-brown lashes fluttered, and she opened her eyes. They widened as she saw her father's face so near, and she raised her arms and put them about his neck. "I love you," she murmured. "I love you so much."

Gethin's reaction was instant and shocking. He pulled the girl's arms down and almost allowed her to fall before he recovered himself. "You must be still, Angharad. You have had a shock. I will carry you home, and you must go to bed until the doctor has seen you. Lie quietly, my dear."

He picked her up and carried her back to the house. Ellen and Miranda followed silently, and Miranda stared at the broad back of her employer as he strode before them. What kind of a father was he who allowed his love for his child to appear only when she was unconscious?

They caught him up when they reached the easier walk across the grass to the house. Angharad lay still making no attempt to touch her father, but her green eyes never left his face and in them was an expression of love and unbearable misery.

Chapter Seven

Angharad's injury was pronounced to be slight by the doctor summoned by boat and pony, and after a day spent resting in bed she was able to resume her activities.

The weather grew warmer until it became unpleasantly hot, and even walking on the shore was no relief since the breeze itself was warm and often carried sand, which stung the face and made the eyes water. But, for Miranda, this was a peaceful time. Her meals were served either in the schoolroom or her bedroom, where a table and chair had been carried. Someone had also made sure that an easy chair was provided so that the room seemed more like a home than any she had known since her parent's death.

In the evenings, when the others were below, spending what both Angharad and Ellen described as "tedious times," Miranda sat at her window until the light faded, fashioning her blue-green and grey materials into a pretty gown.

But Angharad, never in command of herself, grew daily more petulant and difficult. She, Ellen and Miranda had collected many varieties of plants and grasses and pressed them in books. They had collected and washed shells, and Ellen and Miranda sewed the dull materials chosen by Mrs. Mowbray into equally dull dresses for Ellen. Assisted by Miranda, Angharad had tried knitting, embroidery and drawing, but she finished nothing, and one morning sat idly trying to taunt her cousin by making remarks which disparaged the drabness of her attire. Ellen, secure in the knowledge of the silver flowered damask only awaiting her needle, allowed the insults to slide over her and continued to sew placidly.

Angharad then flung out of the schoolroom. The next sounds which reached Ellen and Miranda were the angry raised voice of Gethin and the shrill protestations of Angharad. Flinging down her work, Ellen sped downstairs, to be followed more slowly by Miranda. Once more she felt her position keenly. She was not at all sure whether or not she was expected to keep Angharad in order, or if she would be needed, or desired, at what sounded like a first-class family quarrel.

Since the episode of the storm, Mr. Glendower had treated her with severe courtesy. It was as if that burning embrace had never been, and she felt dismayed at times, as she lay awake in her luxurious bed, to realise that she could not forget his arms about her. Then she would feel unbearably guilty because he was Lora's husband, and if the relationship alone was not enough to shame her, there was the memory of the poor sick woman as she clung to her and begged for friendship.

As she descended the stairs, Mr. Glendower looked up and caught her glance over the head of Angharad, who was facing him. He spoke in rasping tones, "Miranda, cannot you find a way of keeping Angharad occupied? She has just burst into my study, where I was engaged with my bailiff and spoke to me in such a manner . . . ! Cousin Ellen, is there nothing she cares to do?"

Ellen was calm. "It is of no use to blame Miranda or myself, Gethin. We have attempted to instruct my cousin in many useful and pleasurable ways . . ."

"I asked only that we might make an expedition into the hills," cried Angharad. "I am sick of the island. I am hot, always too hot. I want to go where the air is cool on my face. Why can't I? Why?"

"You would do better to ask in more moderate ways," said Ellen.

Angharad was clearly about to answer Ellen with as much insolence as she could muster when Miranda, who now stood between Angharad and her father, intervened hastily. "Mr. Glendower, I know she should speak with more decorum, but truly the past few days have been oppressive. I think it may be thundery. My head has been aching quite often. It is probably affecting Angharad in a similar way. Could you not arrange for her to have a day away from Ynys Yoddfa?"

He looked down into the blue eyes, which stared so pleadingly into his, and his expression softened. "Very well, Miranda, it shall be as you ask." He turned to his daughter. "As for you, Angharad, it would be well for you to learn that soft words and gentle looks do more to gain your ends than does rude behaviour."

She was not listening. She never does, thought Miranda. She seems to see and hear only what she wants, like a spoiled baby. She watched the girl now as she flung herself at her father in an attempt to hug him in gratitude. Gethin stood quite still until Angharad's arms dropped to her sides, then spoke to Ellen and Miranda. "All who want to go on this trip shall do so. We will make it tomorrow. Ellen, perhaps you would ask Mrs. Pritchett to see that a substantial hamper is packed. We will start out early in the morning."

Angharad was in transports of delight and later came bursting into the schoolroom to demand Miranda's immediate attention. Her pleasure in the proposed expedition made her polite. "Please, dear Miranda, will you come to my room with me. I have the prettiest seaside dress of light and dark blue striped surah, which I wore last year when Mama took me with her to Brighton. She thought the sea bathing would improve her health."

"But the sea is at your doorstep," said Miranda, in surprise.

"That is exactly what Mr. Glendower told her, but she would go. She felt that a different coast might be beneficial to her. Do you agree that she was foolish to travel so far, Miranda?"

"I would not presume to criticise anything that your parents did," said Miranda sharply, seeing by the gleam of triumph in Angharad's eyes that the child was trying to lead her into a trap of speaking too candidly.

Angharad seemed to hover once more on the brink of a tantrum, then apparently deciding that her desires mattered more, she took Miranda's hand and pulled her to her feet. "Don't let us quarrel, but come and see why I need you."

The striped frock lay on the bed. Near it was a pair of dark blue stockings and, dragged from a wardrobe, among a jumble of shoes, lay a pair of black and white seaside boots.

Automatically Miranda stopped to tidy the muddle, but again the child tugged at her. "Leave them," she commanded, "one of the maids will do it. Unbutton me and I will show you what has happened."

Miranda helped Angharad out of her dress, and the girl stood in her petticoats and meekly lifted her arms for Miranda to ease on the striped surah. The skirt came to the required length, half-way down her calves, but the bodice was strained against a developed young bosom.

"You see?" said Angharad.

" I perceive that you are becoming a young woman," said Miranda. "Is this frock a favourite of yours? Take it off and I will see what seams may be let out."

Angharad, holding her petticoats out, waltzed around the room. "I am becoming a woman," she sang, "a woman grown and ready for . . . for what, do you suppose, Miranda?"

"I don't know. For happiness, I hope. For mischief if you do not heed the words of those who care for you."

Angharad laughed and again danced round, and Miranda was surprised to see that the child was far more mature of body than had appeared beneath the straight-cut frocks she usually wore. The seams on the striped surah were generous, and after snipping away and fitting it again, she assured the girl that she could make the dress wearable for tomorrow.

Unexpectedly Angharad flung her arms about Miranda and kissed her cheek. "You preach almost as much as my horrid governesses sometimes, but you are kind to me. I do like you."

She could scarcely keep still while Miranda buttoned her back into her former dress and raced out of the room and along the passage to knock and burst immediately afterwards into her mother's room.

"Mama, what do you think?" Miranda heard her cry,

"we are to go tomorrow on an expedition." Then the door slammed, and Miranda winced at the memory of the fragile woman whose head ached often. Tentatively, she knocked on the door and was bidden to enter.

"Please forgive my intrusion," she begged, "but I know that Angharad is very excited. I fear she may distress you with her noise."

Mrs. Glendower was holding her daughter's hand. "Not at all. Angharad comes to see me all too seldom. I am delighted that you are to have a treat, my darling."

"Why don't you come, Mama?"

Instantly the faded woman seemed to draw into a protective shell, and she released Angharad's hand. "You know that is impossible. Go now with Miranda, dearest, I must rest."

Miranda and Angharad walked down the corridor together. "There is nothing the matter with her really, you know, Miranda," remarked the younger girl.

"That is a most unkind thing to say. It is clear that she often suffers. Not everyone is strong and hearty."

"My Mama could be. When she insisted on going to Brighton, Mr. Glendower accompanied us as far as London, where we stayed for two days while she was examined by an eminent doctor in Cavendish Square. I overheard him tell Mr. Glendower that my Mama has no true disease, but was ill for some cause in her mind."

Miranda was horrified. "Angharad, your Mama is easily excited perhaps, but she is quite . . . quite . . ."

"Oh, I don't mean that she is insane or anything like that. She is fretting dreadfully over something, though I cannot tell *you* what it is. I feel sure that Mr. Glendower knows. That is why he is often cross, but I understand him and I shall always care for him. He will see that one day—maybe sooner than you think, and then he will talk to me about Mama and her sick fancies."

"That seems most unlikely, Angharad, and it is clear that you should not have been listening. They cannot have realised that you were within earshot."

"Oh, no, they did not," Angharad assured her complacently. "I was supposed to be downstairs with a perfectly horrid nurse, but she was called away, and I crept upstairs to the waiting place and the door was open between it and the consulting room. Mama was still on the examination couch and could not hear what was said, but I heard, and I know that tomorrow she could rise and join us if she would."

Miranda felt a deepening of pity for Mrs. Glendower. If what her child said was true, then it seemed even more terrible that so little sympathy was given her. The agitation of the emotions could cause real and terrible agony of spirit as Miranda well knew, remembering the loss of her parents. She could not help wondering what sorrow in Mrs. Glendower's life had caused such a deterioration in her health. Was it an unreturned passion for her husband? Miranda could readily imagine how any woman could love such a strong and forceful man as her employer. She jerked her mind from such thoughts and looked down at Angharad, who was pacing beside her, a small secret smile lighting her lovely face.

Ellen and Angharad joined the family for lunch, and Miranda finished hers quickly in the schoolroom. She had threaded her needle to begin the alterations to Angharad's frock when she remembered that there was supposed to be a sewing machine in the house. Presumably Mrs. Pritchett would not consider it necessary to conceal the fact any longer.

Putting aside her resolve never to enter the sewing room again, she began to make her way along passages which grew narrower and darker as she reached the oldest wing. A turn in the corridor brought her face to face with Mrs. Pritchett, and both women stopped.

Miranda considered and rejected several remarks before deciding that silence would best serve her, and she walked on. Mrs. Pritchett did not move, but her cold eyes stayed fixed on Miranda's face as she passed, and she stood absolutely still until Miranda was out of sight.

Feeling intensely thankful that Mrs. Pritchett no longer had power to hurt her, Miranda pushed open the door of the sewing room and a girl, who was seated at the table, turned then rose. She was small, only a little over five feet in height, with a round rosy face and large lustrous dark eyes. The plain cap she wore failed to hide her unruly brown curls, and her perfect teeth showed in a smile which held infectious brightness such as Miranda had not encountered since she left the parsonage. She beamed back, and the girl spoke in a soft sing-song voice in an accent which tinged her English with Welsh and something which Miranda could not define.

"You must be Miss Courtney. I've heard about you from the kitchen. They told me so many stories that I imagined you as a mixture of Delilah and Beelzebub, but I see no horns, and no one could play Delilah in a gown of drab."

The words could have been insulting, but somehow they sounded humorous, and Miranda laughed appreciatively. "I suspect that you are Ceinwen, and I am relieved to find that I did not steal the bread and butter from your mouth after all."

"That Mrs. Pritchett! I should stay away from her if you can. She've got evil inside her if ever I saw it."

Remembering the cold fury of the slate eyes which had transfixed her in the corridor, Miranda shivered. "I came to see if I could borrow the sewing machine," she said, indicating the surah gown. "Miss Angharad has a wish to wear this tomorrow, and it needs letting out at the seams. She is beginning to develop."

"Not before time either."

The words were puzzling and again might have been offensive, but Ceinwen's overpowering warmth and friendliness softened them. "Well, the machine is here, as you see. It was mysteriously returned when I came back. I heard how you sewed without it. Poor soul, I thought, and she probably not used to heavy work and having delicate hands."

Miranda smiled. "Not so delicate, Ceinwen. I was brought up in a parsonage, where we all had to help. May I join you here?"

"That'd be champion." She gurgled with laughter. "Are you perplexed over my way of speaking? Well, I decided that the Welsh hills and valleys didn't need me and went to seek my fortune. My Granny, who reared me, taught me to sew—she was seamstress here—and I got a job in a Lancashire cotton mill. Gran said I'd hate it, and she was right. Those mills are the workshops of Satan. Noise and heat so fierce that some girls worked stripped to the waist. And the wages couldn't keep body and soul together. But I hung on because I wouldn't give Gran the chance to crow over me. She's a wicked old body.

"But I love her, so I do. Then I got word she'd had a turn, and Mr. Glendower sent me money to come home. He's a good one. He pays all the doctor's bills and sends him regular. Gran's heart is tired it seems. Gran thinks the world of her Mr. Gethin."

Ceinwen laughed suddenly. "How I gabble on. Sit yourself down, lass, and use the machine. I'll go on with this bit of hand sewing. I know my English is a bit mixed up because I got most of it from the other lasses in the north. My gran laughs at me."

Miranda joined in Ceinwen's giggle. How glad she was she had come to the sewing room. It seemed like old times when she had worked with the maids at home and exchanged many a joke.

As she threaded the machine she remarked, "I don't think Miss Angharad will be able to wear this much longer. She is young to be growing so fast. I did not begin to look womanly till I was past fourteen." She caught Ceinwen's surprised look. "Have I said something strange?"

"Er, not really, I suppose. I know you've had a confusing time since you came, what with changing your quarters and your position and all, so you won't have had chance to learn much of the family.

"Now I come to think on it, there's probably no one here to tell, my old Gran being the last of the older servants to leave. To tell truth, half the reason I work here is so I can keep her up to date with the family tittle-tattle." Ceinwen's eyes brimmed with laughter. "She've worked here all her days and can't bear to miss anything. And Mr. Glendower pays her a handsome pension, and I could do with being more with her at home."

"I see," said Miranda, thoughtfully. "Yet you manage to encompass both jobs."

"I'm only here a few hours a week, and Mr. Glendower said to allow me to choose my own times. And I don't

101

have to sponge on Gran for food."

Miranda ran up the first seam on the machine and cut and tied the thread. Ceinwen regarded her solemnly. "Have you no curiosity then? Aren't you going to ask what I meant about Miss Angharad?"

Miranda was silent for a while. Again her ambiguous position filled her with bewilderment. She should not gossip with the servants, yet she seemed to be one of them at times. And perhaps if she knew more of Angharad's background, she could help her more effectively.

"Angharad does seem strange to me," she said hesitantly. "I cannot help but feel sorry for her, though it seems silly to do so. She seems to have all she needs."

"Except her father's love!" Ceinwen sounded grim. "Yet once he adored her. No one can understand the change in him."

"Yet the girl herself does not seem puzzled by it," said Miranda. "Hurt often, but not surprised." She was silent again, realising that she had put into words an understanding which had scarcely shaped in her mind. "What *do* you know?" she asked with sudden resolve. "If I can help the girl in any way . . ."

"Miss Angharad was born in the first year of the Glendower marriage," explained Ceinwen simply. "They have been wed these seventeen years."

Miranda felt the chill of shock. "Angharad is what then? Sixteen? I cannot believe it! She can barely read and behaves like . . . like . . ."

"Like the child she is, Miss Courtney. The poor little lass is what is called 'simple'—a bit backward like. I doubt there's any harm in her so long as you treat her like a little 'un."

Miranda, her eyes and hands busy with the frock, worked by instinct as her mind raced. The situation here was more disturbing than she had realised. Angharad possessed a child's understanding in a body which was developing the beauty of a woman and emotions which ranged from babyish to . . . what? They should have told me.

She thought the words had formed only in her mind and was startled when Ceinwen said, "Yes, they might have told you. I understand you're showing that girl a rare help and kindness, and she needs it. All that beauty in a child's mind!"

"Does Mrs. Mowbray know?"

"Oh, yes, Gran says all the relatives came to the wedding from everywhere. It was a grand do, and they say that Mr. Glendower was crazy with love. He was only nineteen, and his bride two years older, and even then 'tis said she was so pale and fragile her father had to support her down the aisle. He meant her to have Mr. Glendower if he had to carry her. He lost his fortune through gaming, and he needed money. Much good it all did him though. He and his wife drowned in a storm as they were crossing the sea to Criccieth."

"How terrible!"

"Yes, and Mrs. Glendower had been ailing since the marriage, and the shock brought on the birth. Angharad was a seven-month baby, so they say, though my naughty Gran winks over that and says she never did hear of an early baby weighing more than eight pounds. But there, Miss Courtney, what of it. They loved a bit too early, but they married. The pity is that they didn't live happily ever after, like story book lovers."

Miranda rose, her face flushed. "I have finished with the machine, thank you, Ceinwen, though I would be grateful if I might borrow it again. I have several gowns to sew."

"Of course, love, and don't be cross with me. Perhaps I spoke too free, but I meant well. You seem just the sort they need here. But I'm glad to go home nights. There's an air about this place that damps me down."

As Miranda passed the drawing room on her way to Angharad's bedroom, she heard the murmur of voices and guessed that the family must be lingering over their coffee. She was startled when the door opened suddenly, and Gethin Glendower walked out. Seeing her, he closed the door and stood for a moment, leaning on it, staring at her as she stopped.

"Busy as always, Miranda? What have you been about?"

"Miss Angharad has a wish to wear this frock tomorrow, sir, and it needed some alteration. She . . . she is growing up."

Something flickered in the depths of his dark eyes as he said, "I fear you are right. She is a problem to me, Miranda, but you are good for her."

He took a step nearer. "You are also far too kind to her. There is no need to make you work on her outgrown clothes. There must be plenty in her wardrobe. I will speak to her."

"No!" The word left her lips involuntarily, and Mr. Glendower raised his brows. Then he gave the smile which wiped the harshness from his face. "Well! My humble little seamstress dares to contradict her master. And why, pray, must I not speak to Angharad?"

"I beg your pardon. I keep forgetting myself . . . it is not easy for me . . . though I do not complain, you comprehend. I am so much more comfortable here now."

"But not happy, eh?"

"Happiness is not the sole aim of the human spirit, sir."

"Spoken like a true daughter of Papa." His smile softened his words, and her lips curved in answer.

"My God, but you're beautiful." His murmur held profound meaning.

"Mr. Glendower, you must not . . ."

"Be silent, Miranda. You are not to be telling me what I must and must not do. I am master here.

"Please don't frown, my dear. I was only teasing. If you feel that to alter Angharad's frocks in some way makes life better, then do so by all means. You seem to have success with her. I have none."

"But she loves you! She needs your kindness so greatly."

His face became harsh, and the lines grew deep. "You speak of matters which are beyond your comprehension. Please excuse me."

He bowed slightly and walked away, and a moment later she heard the main door open and close.

"Upset him, then, haven't you? And fancy him bowing to you like that!"

Miranda whirled round to see Merrick emerging from the shadows. How long had he been there? How much had he heard? She thought of Mr. Glendower's reference to her beauty being bandied about in the servant's hall and coloured.

"My, but you're blushing, Miss Courtney. But you're so pretty that any man would have to tell you of it, and he's a real man for all he neglects his wife. So am I, dear, and I could be of more help to you than him. He's spoken for as the saying is. I'm free and at your service."

Feeling unable to answer Miranda wrenched her gaze from the lascivious grin of the butler and almost ran to Angharad's room, where she laid the seaside frock on the bed.

As she left the room, Bailey approached her along the corridor. "Oh, there you are. Mrs. Glendower sends her compliments, and will you do her the pleasure of attending her?" Her tone and expressive sniff conveyed her opinion of such a plea from a mistress to a maid.

Mrs. Glendower was supported in bed by a number of lacy pillows. She wore a soft knitted shawl of pale green, and her hair was pinned under a cap. She looked white and ill, and Miranda's heart contracted with pity. Why could not anyone see how much she suffered?

"Sit by me, Miranda, that's right, pull up the little chair. You are finding your life supportable here?"

"Oh, yes, indeed, thank you, madam."

Mrs. Glendower smiled faintly. "Do not sound so formal, please. I have already said I look upon you as a friend. I can see your compassion in your face. You are no good at dissembling, are you? You tell everything by your looks."

For an instant Miranda wondered how much of her increasing interest in Gethin Glendower was written plain for all to see, before she crushed the thought. Here, of all places, she must curb her unruly imaginings.

"Miranda, you have been recently in London. I wonder if you have heard any personal accounts of the new electrical treatment."

"Electrical? I have read of it, but I do not properly understand it. And I only passed through London."

"But you may be able to help me." The reedy voice

became petulant. "My husband will not listen to me. I keep showing him pamphlets on the latest methods of cure, but he dismisses them as quackery. But you, my dear, might be able to overcome his objections. He respects you—likes you even—I can tell."

Miranda looked at her searchingly, but there was no malice in Lora's face. She looked pitiful and infinitely in need of love. Her beauty was spoilt, but occasionally one caught a glimpse of what she once had been, maybe could be again if Gethin Glendower cared for his wife. Miranda bit her lip. The assumption about her employer had sprung full-grown into her mind, yet she had no proof. He was abrupt with Lora, impatient of her weakness, but perhaps he was trying to shock her into a response. And love was difficult to define. Miranda supposed that her brother, Walter, would consider love to be the motivation behind pushing his sister towards a marriage with man she detested; love and a desire for her welfare.

Lora had been scrabbling about among a mass of papers and magazines which littered her bed, and she came up now with a leaflet and handed it to Miranda.

"See, it says they can cure nervous disorders as well as physical ones, so my family could have no objection to it. They tell me I suffer with my nerves. Look there: 'Electricity is Life,' and there: 'Galvansim! Nature's Chief Restorer of Exhausted Vital Energy.' What do you think about it, Miranda?"

Lora studied the leaflet again, and Miranda visualised her lying here, day after day, reading one thing after the other, trying to find a cure for something which no one could diagnose. "I do not know about such matters," she answered Lora gently, "but I promise I will approach Mr. Glendower."

After all, what harm could that do, she reasoned with herself? He would likely tell her to mind her own business, but she must risk it. She rose as Lora put a hand to her head. "You are weary. I think I should leave you."

Lora spoke rapidly. "You really are happy here, are you not? And you will stay? You are strong. I sense your strength and your kindness, too."

Miranda looked down into the tired face, and her eyes

you are to breakfast with us today."

She slammed the door, leaving Miranda to dress in a simple dark-blue serge, cut in sporting fashion to the ankles, and the sturdy leather boots which Papa had ordered specially for her to wear on their many long tramps together. Remembering a warning from Ellen that the hills could be cool on even the hottest days, she laid out a plaid wool shawl.

The others were waiting for her, and she made a confused apology for her lateness, but Mr. Glendower smiled as he held her chair. "I judge from Angharad's unusually neat appearance that you have had more than one to tend today. I congratulate you. My wilful child says she hates the attendance of a maid and has had many in hysterics in the past. My cousin, Mrs. Mowbray, has elected to remain behind with Lora so we need not wait breakfast for her."

They were served by Myfanwy and a footman, and Miranda made a good meal of creamy porridge, bacon, eggs and kidneys, and hot rolls. Once she would have been puzzled to know what would happen to the quantities of kedgeree, smoked fish, hams, tongues and devilled chicken, but she could now readily picture the scene below stairs when the food would be passed around until the humblest member would eat what was left. She frowned at the sudden realisation that today that person would be Gwennie and wondered how she would fare at the hands of Mrs. Pritchett.

"Gwennie will not starve for one day."

She looked up, startled into Gethin Glendower's teasing face. "How did you know . . .?"

"Your face conducts your thoughts, Miranda, and I have heard from Mrs. Mowbray, at boring length, that Mrs. Pritchett waxes voluble on the subject of how much food the schoolroom seems to require. She suspects you, I comprehend, of 'over-feeding a work-house brat who doesn't appreciate it and giving her a taste for things above her station.' "

Miranda smiled and found an answering gleam in her employer's dark eyes. For a moment she forgot the others in the magnetism he held for her, but was brought back to her senses by Angharad impatiently scraping back her chair and the demand that they should prepare at once for the journey.

Their ponies awaited them in the stable yard, and Miranda realised, with a sinking spirit, that she was expected to control her mount alone. Dafydd was to accompany them to lead the pack horse laden with rugs and a hamper, and she wished she had been courageous on her arrival at Ynys Nodffa and not pretended to an equestrian skill she lacked.

A stable hand threw her into the saddle and placed the reins in her hand, and the ponies moved out over the pasture to the open sand of the estuary.

The hill tops were still hidden by early mist, but the lower slopes looked invitingly cool with their rich growth of woodland interspersed by rock outcrops. Already the sun was hot, and Miranda felt glad of the protection of her hat. Ellen and Angharad also wore straw bonnets. They provoked Miranda to envy in the way they guided their ponies by an expert flick of the reins or a pressure of a knee. Mr. Glendower led the way on his highbred grey.

They had made their sedate way over half the stretch of sand when Angharad cried, "Oh, how doleful we are," and, kicking her pony's sides, suddenly took off at a gallop. Ellen's mount pranced to one side, and Mr. Glendower's danced and sidled. For an instant the moving body beneath Miranda stiffened, then she found herself clutching desperately at the pommel as her pony raced after its companion. Angharad had left the safety of the path which her father was picking out and seemed to be heading straight for the marshes. Miranda guessed that the girl's knowledge of the terrain would enable her to avoid danger, but she herself was helpless. She dragged at the reins, but having once loosened her hold she now found that the horse was biting firmly on the bit, and it was entirely out of her power to help herself.

Then she heard hoofbeats behind her, a strong hand reached down, and her pony was pulled to a halt. Mr. Glendower was looking at her with an expression of such

110

"She can have it if she wishes. What odds if she does? Last year it was Homoeopathy. She has had every healing woman in the country preparing potions for her. Nothing helps. I tell you, Miranda, her sickness is within her. I would help her if I could."

He dug his heels into his horse's sides, and they moved up the hill faster, but he did not forget to control her pony.

The road grew rougher as they left the scattered dwellings until it petered out altogether into a track. Mr. Glendower led them out of the forest into sunlight and heathland, where the ponies picked their way delicately through bracken and rock. They splashed through streams which trickled and tumbled to the river, and occasionally a startled sheep turned and trotted away, its stumpy tail wagging furiously, making Angharad laugh.

Ellen had not spoken since they left Mrs. Morgan's cottage, but she looked around her wonderingly, and her light blue eyes shone as she drank in the beauty of their surroundings. At last the track led them to the shore of a lake, and they stopped and dismounted.

While Dafydd and Mr. Glendower tethered the ponies, Miranda and Ellen kept a watch on Angharad as she ran about in delight at her freedom, revelling in the cool breeze, which ruffled the lake's placid surface, and filling her hands with wild flowers.

Returning to Miranda, she thrust the tangled bunch into her arms. "Look Miranda, bedstraw! And smell the Grass-of-Parnassus, it has the scent of honey, and fern, and here is St. John's wort. Look at the leaves. They are heart-shaped. Would you care to have a leaf, Cousin Ellen, then you could wear it on your sleeve, could you not? Or if you broke your heart, you could use it to stop the bleeding! Did you know that folk believe it to have such magical properties?"

"You seem to know a deal about the flowers here," said Miranda. "Perhaps you would be kind enough to teach me."

"Oh, I am no school marm! My Mama used to bring me here a long time ago, and someone who came with us knew all about the plants."

"Do you mean Mrs. Morgan?"

"Oh, no, not her! I refer to Nanny Powys, my Mama's old nurse. She accompanied my Mama when she came to Ynys Noddfa, and we had good times together. But now she is no longer there. I miss her." The child's face crumpled, and Miranda thought she was about to weep and said gently, "I expect she was old when she died, dear. I'm sure she had been happy with you and Mrs. Glendower

Angharad gave a harsh laugh. "Nanny Powys is not dead! She would not stay at Ynys Noddfa. She said she could not bear to see her dear Miss Lora so ill-used as she was. But I think Mr. Glendower sent her away. He thought she encouraged Mama to imagine herself ill. Or perhaps she knew more than he liked about our family matters. She lives in the hills about the village. Would you care to visit her?"

"I doubt if Miranda would find such a visit edifying, Angharad." Mr. Glendower had joined them and sounded angry.

"I do not suppose she would, but she might find it very interesting."

Her father frowned and Miranda said quickly, "Angharad, it is a pity you picked the flowers so early in the day. They will die unless we care for them."

"Let them die," answered the girl carelessly. "I can pick more. There are plenty."

"That would be wrong, dear. Look at the moss growing near the lake. If we wrap it round the stems and leave the plants in the shade they will stay fresh."

Angharad shrugged. "As you please, though it seems a lot of silly fuss to me."

Seeing Mr. Glendower's face darken with displeasure at his daughter's impertinence, Miranda began to walk rapidly towards the lake. She was stopped by her employer, who caught her up and laid his hand on her arm. "Not so fast. It is very marshy near the lake-side."

His glance followed hers down, and he laughed. "What sensible footwear for a young lady! Right, we will go together."

The ground squelched beneath their weight, but by

ended their meal with a Chocolate Cream and retired to the drawing room, leaving Mr. Glendower to enjoy his port wine. Mrs. Mowbray pounced at once.

"Miranda Courtney, you have paint on your face!"

Miranda smiled. "Not paint, Mrs. Mowbray, I assure you. The sun caught my nose, and I have put on a little glycerine and rose-water. And . . ."—she grinned, forestalling the next outburst—"the merest touch of Rachel face powder to conceal the oiliness. That is not painting my face."

"It is all the same to me! How you have the brazen effrontery to appear at the dinner table, and before two innocent young ladies, like a . . . a . . . painted Jezebel . . ."

"How dare you!" Miranda's voice was icy. "I will not—cannot—permit *anyone* to address me in such a fashion. If Papa countenanced my use of a little powder then it must be all right."

"I am surprised that a parson should be so lax in his ways!"

Miranda's voice shook a little as she tried to control her indignation. "My papa was never lax. He was a good man—a fine man!"

Ellen interposed, "Mama, those are strong words. We would not care to have our own dear Papa spoken of in so ill a manner."

Mrs. Mowbray breathed deeply. "Miranda, I may have been a little—precipitate—in my choice of expression. I had not intended to speak badly of the dead, but I am honest when I say that I do not understand your father's views."

"I apologise for my impertinence," said Miranda evenly. "You see, my Papa admired the writer Mrs. Mary Haweis, who was the wife of a famous preacher and unimpeachably respectable. She advocated that it is sinful not to make the best of the looks which God has given us and that the modest use of cosmetics could not harm the moral fibre. We are, I think, all entitled to our point of view."

Whatever Mrs. Mowbray might have said was lost as Merrick entered, followed by a footman and a maidservant who brought in coffee and placed it at Mrs. Mowbray's elbow. She poured and Merrick served and the conversation was kept commonplace.

Mr. Glendower joined them and suggested a little music, and while Miranda played the piano, he and Ellen sang, his rich Welsh baritone blending with Ellen's thin, but sweet, soprano. Later, Angharad played a piece with slap-dash carelessness before she retired, leaving the others to talk in a desultory fashion until half-past ten, when Mrs. Mowbray announced that it was time for the ladies to go to their beds.

They were on their way to the door when it burst open, and Angharad darted into the room. She wore her night-gown and wrapper, but her feet were bare, her face white and terrified, and her eyes enormous. "Mama is ill, oh, so very ill. Please do fetch a doctor. Miss Bailey says it is imperative and so does Mrs. Pritchett."

Mr. Glendower strode past her saying, "I will see. Do nothing yet."

Moments later they heard him in the hall shouting for someone to go instantly for a doctor before he re-entered the room. "She is indeed ill. There can be no doubt this time. Miranda, she calls for you. I know you are no nurse, but if you could . . ."

"Of course I will." She left with Mrs. Mowbray's indignant protestations following her.

Lora's face was twisted in agony as she writhed in her bed, and Bailey and Myfanwy ran to-and-fro as the sick woman retched constantly. When she saw Miranda, she tried to speak, but another bout of anguished torment seized her, and she stared at the girl with eyes dark with pain. Miranda sank to her knees by the bed and took Lora's hands in hers. "Dear Mrs. Glendower, do not try to speak. I will stay as long as you want me."

She took the damp cloth from the bedside table and wiped Lora's brow and whispered words of courage to her. The maids continued to bring clean bowls until it seemed impossible for anyone to continue in such violent spasms. Eventually the sickness and purging receded and Lora lay back, her face deathly pale, her lids and hands twitch-ing. Miranda felt a touch on her shoulder and turned her head to see Mr. Glendower holding a small chair for her. She rose from her knees and sat down, surprised to find how cramped she was from her long vigil.

She still held Lora's hands, and once the sick woman opened her eyes, which glowed feverishly in pools of darkness, smiled wanly at Miranda and finally fell into an exhausted sleep.

The doctor arrived and gently examined Lora, who refused to allow Miranda to leave so that she saw for the first time how truly emaciated Lora's body had become. Her bones seemed almost to stick through her skin, and at the end of his gentle probing the doctor shook his head and tutted. "Poor lady! She would not be able to withstand many such attacks."

He then began to confer with Mr. Glendower, and Miranda could hear their murmuring voices as they walked from the bedroom, leaving her to sit quietly in the darkened room, still holding Lora's limp hands. Bailey moved quietly about putting the room in order, and once, when their glances met, Miranda was shaken to see the jealous malevolence in the maid's eyes.

Myfanwy returned to summon Miranda to the master's study, and she slid her hands from Lora's and rose. "Call me at once, please, if she wants me," she whispered to Bailey, who did not reply.

In the study the doctor was seated with a glass of brandy in his hand while Mr. Glendower paced up and down, a look of cold fury on his face.

"Ah, Miranda. Doctor Jenkins believes that everyone should be questioned about my wife's illness. He seems to think that there is something sinister about it."

His scornful voice provoked the other man to red-faced anger. "I tell you, sir, that I know nothing, that there has never been anything in your wife's condition which would account for such a violent attack as she has just suffered. If it had continued, it must have destroyed her."

He looked at Miranda. "You are Miss Courtney, I take it. I have questioned the kitchen staff, who all swear that nothing was sent from there to Mrs. Glendower which could upset her. Apparently, the meat and cauliflower with which she was served, were eaten by you all. I have been informed, by Mrs. Pritchett, that you possess an unusual knowledge of poisonous substances. Have you any fresh light to throw upon the matter?"

"What is this about poisons?" Mr. Glendower's voice was harsh. "What kind of talk is this? What are you suggesting, Doctor Jenkins?"

"I suggest nothing," replied the doctor, but his eyes darted from Miranda to Mr. Glendower in speculation. "I have only a few facts, and I am not given to drawing fanciful conclusions. But surely, as the husband of the lady in question, you are vitally concerned with learning the truth."

"The truth is that my wife heard before dinner that Angharad and the rest of us had picnicked in the spot where she and . . . in short, a place which holds memories for her of which you are well aware. It is my belief that she excited herself into an emotional sickness."

The doctor took a sip of brandy. "I would not deny that Mrs. Glendower has, in the past, suffered from many an attack of nervous disorders, but you must recognise that this was different." He held up his hand to forestall further argument. "Allow me to know my profession, sir."

Mr. Glendower subsided into angry silence while the doctor said, "Now, Miss Courtney, if Mrs. Glendower ate only what you all enjoyed, then she cannot have taken harm from so doing. Therefore, we must look deeper for the cause of her sickness. There is emphatically no organic reason for the attack, so it follows that she must have eaten or drunk some injurious matter. Can you think of anything—anything at all?"

"Surely Bailey would know more of my wife's actions," interposed Mr. Glendower. "She should be the one to interrogate!"

Again the doctor's look was speculative. "I intend to see her, if it becomes necessary. Miss Courtney, I have already explained to your employer that it is imperative for me to discover the cause of his wife's illness as she may need further urgent treatment."

Miranda suddenly recalled an incident earlier in the day and her expression was not lost on the doctor. "You have thought of something, I believe."

Chapter Ten

During the next days Lora slowly recovered her strength. Autumn came kindly with soft breezes and gentle sunshine. The distant hills were purple and gold with heather and the deepening yellow of the bracken, and morning mists, dispelled by the sun, reminded them of the approach of winter.

Lora decided that she could not cancel the birthday party, which friends and tenants had always expected from the ladies of Ynys Noddfa, and she began to struggle to sit out of bed for longer times each day, though it hurt Miranda to see how she had to fight for determination. The two women spent more time together, and Lora seemed to find great help in the vital presence of her new friend.

Miranda had also largely taken over the care of Angharad and, by using tact and persuasion, had actually caused her to finish one or two water colours and to knit a simple watch case for her father. The girl's face glowed with pride as she handed it to him, and he looked from her to Miranda in a puzzled fashion. "You made this entirely by yourself, Angharad?"

"Yes, I did! I had no help, did I, Miranda? Do not you think it a pretty case? Will you promise me to wear it?"

Her voice had taken on the feverish eagerness with which she so often addressed him, and Miranda held her breath as she saw how Mr. Glendower frowned in distaste. For an instant she felt afraid that he would refuse the gift, and words of anger had begun to form in her mind before he smiled with the charm which robbed his face of harshness and said, "Thank you, Angharad. I will wear it and I am truly grateful."

Angharad's beautiful face lit with joy, and she stepped towards her father with the clear intention of embracing him, but he moved a little back, took his daughter's hands in his and brushed her cheek with a brief kiss, then walked swiftly away. His daughter watched him go with a bleak expression, and Miranda wondered yet again why a man who seemed so sensitive to her own needs should be so blind where his child was concerned.

She had made no promise to stay at Ynys Noddfa, but as yet she had formed no plans to move, and Mr. Glendower did not press her for a definite statement of intent. It seemed that they were both willing to let matters ride for a while.

With the advent of a party Ellen and Miranda had to speed their preparations for their gowns, and toiled secretly over the green-blue and grey silks and the blue and silver Damassin. To satisfy Mrs. Mowbray the girls had to make up the boring ochre poplin, and, to add to Miranda's growing responsibilities, Lora had produced a black-velvet gown from her closet and requested Miranda to take in the seams to fit her thinner frame.

Fortunately Mrs. Mowbray was content to wear one of her plain black silks, and Angharad's green velvet, made only the previous Christmas and worn once, still fitted her. "The seamstress who sewed it had not your skill, Miranda," exclaimed Angharad, "and it was a little too large. *She* said that children's clothes should always be made big for them to grow into—as if I were a poor village nobody, but it fits me well now, does it not?" The ankle length emerald velvet deepened the hue of her eyes and made a satisfying contrast with her titian hair. It also lent her a certain maturity, and Miranda felt deeply disturbed at the sight of so immature a mind captured in so much beauty.

Somehow it was now taken for granted that Miranda join the family for dinner each night, although she still took lunch in the schoolroom. This meant that much of the sewing must be done at night. Ceinwen had been let into the secret of the new gowns and smilingly helped with the seams on her machine, but the hand sewing was completed by Ellen and Miranda after the others had retired. In the secrecy of Miranda's bedroom the two girls whispered of their lives and hopes, and Miranda daily grew fonder of Ellen and felt sorrier than ever for her as there seemed small prospect of Ellen ever acquiring the husband and home for which she longed. But mostly Ellen was cheerful and showed a down-to-earth sense, which came as welcome relief in this house of jagged emotions.

When Miranda went to the sewing room one lunch time with Ellen's gown concealed in a piece of linen, Ceinwen greeted her with her usual bright smile then said, "My Gran wants to know how Mrs. Glendower is. She's had a visit from Nanny Powys. The old lady walked all the way from the hills nearly over by Harlech though 'tis said she's almost ninety. She nursed Miss Lora's mother, too."

"What did Nanny Powys want?"

Ceinwen shrugged. "You know how gossip spreads, and it's all over the place that Mrs. Glendower had some sort of attack, and people are saying she was poisoned. The old woman has got it into her head that her beloved lady is in danger. It's the first time she's come out of the hills since she left Ynys Noddfa. If someone could give her a comforting message, it might stop that gabby tongue of hers."

Miranda bit her lip. "Do people believe what they hear, Ceinwen?"

"You know what folk are like, miss. They like to think the worst, or pretend they do. Some of the women enjoy shivering as they talk of poisons and witch's brew and such things. My dear old Gran is the most harmless woman alive, and people come for miles for her cures, yet there are some who call her a witch. If she is, then she's a white one."

"But surely no one connects your grandmama with Mrs. Glendower's illness!"

"No one had better say so to my face," cried Ceinwen. She continued more calmly. "But Nanny Powys has some crazy tale of Mr. Glendower visiting Gran's cottage on

the day his wife was taken bad and Nanny Powys asked
if he had collected any poison."

"This is terrible! All we procured was some corn oint-
ment for Mrs. Mowbray! The doctor thinks that the
mushrooms were to blame."

"That's true I'm sure, if you say so, but if someone
were to set Nanny Powys's mind easy it might stop her
wagging tongue."

"I will speak to Mr. Glendower and he . . ."

"No, that you must not! Mrs. Powys hates him! If
he went to see her, it would make things worse."

"Hates him! But, why?"

"No one really knows. I think my Granny might be
able to tell something, but she won't. It has to do with
the past. Anyway, most folk think Mrs. Powys isn't right
in the head, so maybe they won't take too much heed
of her."

Miranda stared at Ceinwen. "But who can see her
then? Who can stop these terrible rumours?"

"Well, miss, there's one who Mrs. Powys loves as much
as her Miss Lora and that's Miss Angharad. Perhaps if
you and Miss Ellen were to take the girl to visit her, she
could set her mind easy about her mam. It would be
worth a try."

"But what excuse can I make?"

"I can't help you there. I expect you'll think of something."

Miranda began to work on Ellen's gown, and in her
agitation, inserted stitches in the wrong place, and the
lunch time was wasted while she unpicked. She was still
preoccupied when Ellen and Angharad rejoined her in
the schoolroom, and after trying vainly to make her talk,
Angharad flew into a bad mood and became spiteful.
She began to taunt her cousin with her lack of fortune.
"Your papa cannot have been as wise as mine! My papa
knows best how to use his wealth."

Ellen answered evenly. "My papa was misled into
making unsafe investments. He was not . . . not perhaps
a very clever man of business, though a good and dear
father to me."

"That does not gain a woman a dowry, which she

needs to marry, especially if she is not endowed with looks."

Miranda looked up quickly. Ellen's face had coloured, and her lips were pressed tightly together.

"Miss Angharad, you should know better than to speak with such insolence to your cousin, who has shown you nothing but kindness."

Angharad shrugged and returned to her painting, dipping her brush into a paint pot and withdrawing it so carelessly that a large yellow blob landed in the middle of the sky. "Oh, how tiresome! See what I have done, Miranda! I was painting the entrance to Mr. Glendower's mine and wanted to put a clump of Welsh poppies in the picture. They grow there in abundance. I picked some once when I went to see Nanny Powys. She lives near by."

Miranda's brain raced. "I should like very much to see your Papa's mine. Is one permitted to enter it? I have never seen a mine of any kind."

Angharad dropped her brush and clapped her hands. "That's a capital idea. Yes, we can go into the upper tunnels if we are properly conducted, though we are not allowed in the lower tunnels—it is too dangerous. I will ask Mr. Glendower if we may go."

"And perhaps we could combine the outing with a visit to your old nurse," suggested Miranda, "she would like that, I think."

"Oh, yes, I daresay she would," answered Angharad carelessly. "Yes, I suppose we would have to do that. I will ask Mr. Glendower now about seeing the mine, and I will look in the tide chart. We may need a boat arranged."

She darted away, slamming the door behind her, and Ellen allowed her sewing to fall to her lap and her hands to lie idle. She stared ahead, and Miranda saw pain in the light eyes, as she said flatly, "Angharad is cruel, but she is right, you know, Miranda. I need a dowry to become a married woman."

"Oh, don't speak so, Ellen. You have never had a fair chance from all I hear—and you *can* attract a man. Remember the day on the mountain—the young farmer —what was his name? Huw Craddock! He seemed to

". . . to . . ." She stopped, realising that to remind Ellen of the admiration of one who was lower in station than herself was scarcely likely to help her.

"He seemed to what?" prompted Ellen softly.

Miranda did not answer, and Ellen continued. "He found me pleasing, did he not, Miranda? He liked my looks and I liked his—but I know it would not do. And yet . . . yet I felt drawn to him."

The girls sat in a silence which was interrupted by Angharad's noisy entry. "Mr. Glendower says we may go tomorrow, and Dafydd will accompany us. Mr. Glendower regrets not being able to come, but he has meetings with tenant farmers planned for several days and says it is too late to put them off. He will not let them gather only to be disappointed. He says it would be a waste of their time. Only think—he is so thoughtful for such low people. Is not he a good and splendid man! Though I would so much rather he came with us . . ."

Her gaiety died away abruptly, and in her need to comfort Angharad, Miranda found it easier to stifle her own disappointment that her employer could not take the trip with them.

Miranda woke early the next day to find the sun rising in a beautiful misty September dawn. The day would be fine, and they would be able to make their visit to the mine. She had no clear idea of what to say to Nanny Powys or, indeed, how to broach the subject of Mrs. Glendower's attack, but she felt she must make some move to try to quell the rumours. Gethin Glendower might not love his wife as he should, but Miranda found it impossible to believe that he would ever stoop to hurting her.

Dafydd led the ponies across the stretch of sand and safely through the marshy path to the lane, where Miranda was surprised and pleased to find that a gig awaited them, already harnessed to a sturdy horse.

Angharad explained, "We take the coast road for some way, and Mr. Glendower has laid a road to our mine for the horses to drag down the carts of slate. We can walk the short way over the hills to Nanny Powys, so today we ride in comfort and elegance.

"You will like that won't you, Miranda," she teased, her green eyes sparkling. "Poor seamstress who cannot really ride at all."

But she was too excited to be malicious and soon forgot everything in pointing out the glorious view of the coast far below them as they followed the road, which climbed the hills. Above them, stretched the forest, where they caught glimpses of mossy clearings, or tumbling streams on their way to the sea. Miranda was soothed and enchanted by the beauty around her and almost forgot the worrying nature of her purpose in coming out.

Dafydd led the horse as they began the steep climb to the slate mine. Trees gave way to bracken and heather, and the rocky outcrops grew more numerous until suddenly ahead of them appeared the mouth of the mine, looking like a dark gash in the side of the hill. The entrance was flanked by cutting sheds from which proceeded the rhythmic sound of a steam engine, and slate waste spilled down the hillside.

"It is so ugly!" exclaimed Ellen, then looking quickly at Angharad's face, which had darkened with anger, she finished, "but so necessary, I do comprehend. Without such work the local men and their families might go hungry, and slate is essential to the extensive building nowadays."

Both she and Miranda were relieved when Angharad's face cleared, and she laughed and clapped her hands in glee as the gig stopped and Dafydd helped them down, before removing the harness and leading the horse to a hitching post near a water trough. "I think it would be best if we go to see Mrs. Powys first," he suggested in his gentle lilting tones. "The sun's promising to grow hot later, and there's little shade. The mine can wait awhile."

In spite of Angharad's pout this was agreed, and the four of them began the steep ascent up a rough track, Dafydd sometimes giving them the support of his strong arm.

Miranda paused to regain her breath. "How does an old lady manage to get up and down a place like this?" she marvelled.

Dafydd grinned. "That one's like a mountain sheep.

Born and bred here she was, her father being a shepherd, and she only left when times grew hard. She went into service with Mrs. Glendower's family and was a quick learner and good with little ones they say. She was the eldest of eleven so I reckon she'd plenty of practice. She became a nursery maid and worked her way to Head Nurse. She stayed with Mrs. Glendower when she married the master until . . . well . . . she took it into her head that her beloved lady was being mistreated and made herself so obnoxious that Mr. Glendower had to tell her to leave. She's never forgiven him. I think she'd do him a mischief if she could, but what could the likes of her do to an important man like him?"

What indeed? thought Miranda, but perhaps the rejected old woman held more power than anyone realised. Gossip had been known to destroy people.

After twenty minutes of steady climbing, Miranda realised that what she had taken to be an outcrop of rock overlaid with withered bracken was actually a low stone dwelling with a thatched roof. The straw was ragged in places, and the house looked grim even on this bright day. Miranda wondered what it was like in the winter as the winds screamed across the hillside, and she shivered.

The occupant had evidently heard their approach, for the door opened and a woman appeared, staring down the hill, shading her eyes with grimy hands. She was of medium height and very thin. Her face was deeply wrinkled, and her iron-grey hair drawn back and skewered in a knot. She wore a black gown, rent about the hem and rusty with age. As the party drew near, Miranda saw that her eyes were fixed upon Angharad with yearning in their dark, red-rimmed depths, and as the girl reached her she put out trembling hands and laid them on Angharad's shoulders. She tried to pull her close, but Angharad jerked her head aside, and the kiss, aimed at her lips, landed on the bright auburn hair. Her lips moved in what were clearly endearing terms in her own musical language, then she switched to English and murmured, "My little flower. You're the image of your mama. Just as she was at your age. How is she? How is my treasure?"

Dafydd said, "Good morning, Mrs. Powys," and his

voice seemed to pull her back from some distant vision, and her face took on a malignant look as her eyes roamed over the two young women.

"I've heard of you. You'll be *his* cousin—and you're the beautiful one who've come to sew. How many more will arrive at Ynys Noddfa waiting to step into my darling's shoes? But she shan't die! She shan't! She'll laugh at you all yet. I've been to Harlech and told the police inspector about how people are trying to hurt Miss Lora. So if anything happens to her he'll know all about it."

The words were an outrage to the three elder members of the party and to the innocence of the happy, sunny day they had been enjoying, and for a moment nobody moved. Then Dafydd, whose face was crimson, said quietly. "She's having one of her bad days. Perhaps we ought to go back. I don't know what Mr. Glendower would say if . . ."

Miranda interrupted him smoothly. "No, Dafydd, she is very old and clearly loves Mrs. Glendower, and Angharad, too. It would be cruel simply to walk away."

"Miranda is right," agreed Ellen. "May we come in, Mrs. Powys? It is a long climb from the mine, and we are hot and thirsty."

The old woman's face crumpled as if she might weep, then she took Angharad's hand. "Come, my pretty. You and your friends shall have a sup of dandelion wine."

It took Miranda's eyes a few moments to adjust to the darkness of the one-roomed house which was lighted only by a small window. Her eyes began to water, and she saw that the hearth was in the centre of the room and the peat smoke drifted to the blackened thatch. A steaming pot hung from a single firedog, adding to the thick atmosphere, and an unlit rush light was suspended from the roof.

Angharad giggled. "You will have to sit on one of the benches. The smoke doesn't linger down there."

Miranda obeyed and found the air clearer near the ground. She stared at the fire, which was backed by a large stone. Mrs. Powys was clattering at the dresser; Dafydd had elected to stay outside, and Ellen joined Miranda on the bench. She murmured, "Cousin Gethin told me that in these old cottages, so long as the fireback stone remains standing, no one may take possession of a person's house, however long they stay away. When Nanny Powys left the island, she returned here and claimed the family dwelling. Now the fire never goes out."

Miranda's eyes were more accustomed to the dimness, and she stared as she saw that what she had taken for a cupboard was the end of a box bed on which shelves had been built. A platform of slate slabs raised a long case clock and the food cupboard from the dirt floor. This, and a couple of benches, seemed to compose all the old woman's chattels.

She came towards them carrying a tray on which there were three tumblers containing a clear liquid. Miranda wondered if Ellen would decline refreshment since the place could scarcely be described as hygienic, yet the tumblers were sparklingly clean, and it appeared that Nanny Powys had not forgotten all that she had learned in her long years in gentlemen's households. Both girls took a tumbler and sipped appreciatively at the wine, which had a pleasant flavour. Ellen put out a restraining hand in an attempt to prevent Angharad from emptying her brimming glass, but the girl pushed the hand away and continued to drink.

Nanny Powys squatted close to Angharad, fixing the others with her dark eyes. "You've come for a purpose," she stated flatly. Miranda wondered if it were possible to keep secrets from this woman.

"I heard that you were concerned for Mrs. Glendower," she answered. "Mr. Glendower has allowed us to pay a visit to the slate mine, and we decided that we would see you first to make your mind easy."

"So *he* doesn't know you're then?"

"No, but I feel sure that he would have desired us to . . ."

"He would never have let you come here. He's a hard, cruel man is that one . . ."

Angharad sprang to her feet. "If you say bad things about Mr. Glendower I shall leave instantly!"

Mrs. Powys rose with surprising haste and put her claw-like hands on Angharad's arms. "Now, siwgr wyn,

146

I don't mean to say anything to upset you. I wouldn't harm a hair of your head, would I? Now sit down, my angel, and let your old Nanny look at you some more."

Angharad sank back, pouting, and sipped at her wine. Some had slopped to the ground, and Ellen muttered, "That's a good thing, Miranda. This is potent—far more so than you realise, I think."

"Tell me about your mama," begged Mrs. Powys. "I heard she was poisoned. Is it true? Who did it to my dear little lady?"

"If she was poisoned, it was an accident," said Ellen, but the old woman ignored her and listened intently to Angharad.

"Mama had a bad attack. She suffered from a good deal of purging. The doctor thought she must have eaten something which disagreed with her. That is all, Nanny, I swear."

"Something she ate, eh? Oh, I don't doubt that there are some who would wish her gone. Mabi del i—my pretty baby!" She rocked herself back and forth, squatting on her heels, holding her arms about her stomach, her voice a thin whine. Miranda and Ellen looked at one another and rose.

"We must be leaving now, Mrs. Powys," said Ellen, but the old woman was lost in her memories and continued to rock and wail.

Miranda felt defeated. She had hoped to be able to quell, at source, the rumours which she felt convinced were begun by this woman, but it was clear that she was past understanding the difference between truth and the evil surmise generated by her hatred of Gethin Glendower. She walked out into the sunlight, where Ellen joined her, and together they watched a falcon circling the sky, to swoop and rise, with a helpless victim in its claws.

Angharad appeared a few moments later. She was flushed and talked rapidly in a high excited voice. "Nanny Powys loves my mama and me, but I don't think she cares for anyone else. I have just told her that she must not say naughty things about Mr. Glendower, because we love him whatever has happened, and no one must think ill of him."

"Nothing *has* happened," said Miranda sharply. "Nothing," she amended, "which should cause your old nurse, or anyone, to speak badly of . . . of any person. There was an accident. That is all. Is not that so?"

"Of course it is." Angharad danced away from the others and began the descent, her feet scarcely touching the path in places. She refused all aid and leapt, without fear, from small crags, to land in the bracken and grass below.

"She's *tipsy*," said Ellen. "She should never have been offered dandelion wine. That foolish old woman is besotted by Cousin Lora and her daughter. She cannot see beyond them."

They reached the mouth of the slate mine and rested, partaking of the cool lemonade packed by Mrs. Rhys. Then, led by the mine manager, and accompanied by Dafydd, they entered the dark opening in the hillside.

Miranda quickly understood why Mr. Glendower had advised them to take warm shawls. The first level was fairly warm from the light and air, which came from a large vent cut through the solid rock and through which they could see the sky, but when they began to walk carefully down the rocky steps to the second level, the cold struck shiveringly at them. Dafydd and the manager held lamps and so did Angharad, she having begged for one, saying she felt nervous in the dark.

She, however, showed no sign of nerves, and several times the manager was forced to call her back. "Miss Angharad," he implored, "you must not, indeed, you must not wander off. There are sudden drops where you could fall. The men have to climb to deeper levels by the steepest of ways, and you could be gravely hurt." But Angharad only laughed and disobeyed until Ellen insisted on holding her firmly by the hand.

They watched, fascinated, as the rockmen hammered in the long iron rods, making the holes into which they would insert gunpowder to shift another slate block. The manager told them that far below their feet the miners were digging and widening further chambers wherever the slate veins led them. "But we shan't be going there, ladies. It is too perilous, and the air is thick with slate dust."

Miranda thought of men toiling away, the blackness relieved only by the mutton-fat candles, which increased the foulness of the air. Even here, where the chambers were lofty and the air reasonably fresh, the stench of the candles was, at times, overpowering.

They continued to walk through caverns supported by thick slate pillars left intact by the miners. The manager explained, "Mr. Glendower says that the slate is five hundred million years old in these pillars. Fancy it waiting all that time for us to find and slate our roofs. He knows a lot about such things. He's a good man as well as clever. He's had narrow-gauge lines laid to haul out the slate. It's back-breaking work, is digging out slate, I won't deny that, but it must be done, you see, and he pays us good money."

They paused to watch a rockman high above them on an almost sheer wall. He hung by a chain which was wound around his thigh and threaded through an iron peg which he had driven into the rock. Miranda wondered how he found it possible to see by the infinitesimal light thrown by his single candle, and in her absorption she failed to notice that Angharad was no longer with them, until she glanced at Ellen, who, also engrossed, had loosened her hold upon the girl.

Miranda glanced quickly about her and caught a glimmer of a lamp down one of the corridors. Without pausing to consider, she sped after it and was in time to see Angharad peering into the inky blackness of a deeper level.

"Look, Miranda, there are steps cut into the rock and a rope for the men to hold. Should you not like to descend and explore?"

"No, I would not, Angharad, and you are naughty and wilful to run off in this fashion. You could be severely hurt, and even if you care nothing for yourself, you might stop to remember that if your Papa heard of this he could be angry with his workmen for their supposed carelessness."

Angharad laughed. "You must not be afraid, seam-

stress. You must fear nothing, least of all must you fear
Mr. Glendower. Hs is good and wonderful and one day
he and I will . . . well, I will not tell you my secrets
yet, but one day you will all be surprised." She swung
the lantern to-and-fro, and their shadows danced crazily
over the walls and roofs. "I will never fear anything. See!"

Without warning she opened the glass panel in the lamp
and blew, and they were plunged into a blackness Miranda
could scarcely credit. She thought of the yawning hole
near their feet. The darkness seemed to press upon her,
and she felt panic rise in her throat. I must not give way,
she thought, I must not.

"Angharad," she called, "where are you?"

There was utter stillness, and Miranda felt she must
be in a nightmare. Where was the girl? She could not
have fallen. She would have screamed. Surely she would
have screamed.

"Angharad, please," she begged.

The girl's voice came softly through the darkness.
"Poor little seamstress. You are afraid, but you must
not be. Nothing could harm us in Mr. Glendower's own
mine. Who would dare to hurt us?"

"Angharad, no one would do us harm, I know, but
remember the awful drop so near. If we move we could
fall. I cannot remember how far I am from it. The
darkness—it confuses me . . ."

She heard her voice break on a sob and tried to hang
on to her calm, but Angharad, infected perhaps by
Miranda's fear, suddenly cried out and launched herself at
her companion. They collided and staggered, and Miranda
struggled to remain upright, but her foot slipped and for
a terrible second she knew they were poised at the very
brink of the chasm. She regained her balance, launched
herself and Angharad in the opposite direction, and they
both fell to the ground, Angharad sobbing loudly in
Miranda's arms.

Anxious voices called their names, blessed light
appeared, and they were escorted from the mine by a
white-faced manager. Over and over he apologised until
Miranda, pitying his fears which must be not only for
them, but for the fact that perhaps he would lose his

position and leave himself and family without support, said firmly, "It was not your fault and if anything is said I will tell Mr. Glendower so, you may rest assured."

They climbed into the gig, their spirits depressed by the events of the morning. Miranda felt she would gladly return at once to Ynys Noddfa, but Dafydd turned the horse into a sunny glade at the foot of a waterfall and suggested gently that they rest and eat lunch. Miranda did not feel hungry, but when Ellen unpacked the crusty rolls, butter and cheese, apple tart and cream, Morello cherries and claret cup, her normal healthy appetite reasserted itself. Angharad hankered after the wine until Ellen showed her that Mrs. Rhys had packed a small packet of sherbet and a bottle of water for her.

The girl exclaimed with delight as Ellen tipped the powder into the water. "See how it fizzes and bubbles. It sparkles in the sun. Oh, it is almost too pretty to drink!"

Miranda watched her. She seemed to have entirely forgotten the past hours in her amusement. More and more she seemed like the child which Ceinwen said she was, but surely even quite small children had more command over their emotions than Angharad seemed to possess. Miranda wondered if it was the unbearable knowledge of her daughter's immaturity which caused Lora to hide herself away in her room. She felt her spirits sink and longed to be back in her bedroom to have time to ponder. If I left the island, she thought, Lora would soon forget me. She is almost as much a child as her daughter at times. And Gethin Glendower? He must forget, too, and she must put all memory of him from her. Yet the idea of turning her back on Ynys Noddfa hurt her with the sharpness of a knife turning in a wound.

She heard Ellen give a soft exclamation and looked up. Approaching them through the glade was Huw Craddock. He and his pony seemed as one in their handsome ruggedness, and Miranda saw with a pang how Ellen's eyes held a light which caused their blue depths to glow and how the colour flooded her delicate complexion.

The farmer dismounted and threw the reins over a low branch. He nodded to Dafydd and stood looking down at the picnickers. He was bareheaded and light filtered by the trees gave golden glints to his hair. He bowed. "You have a lovely day for your feast. It is well to make the most of the sun. Winter will be upon us all too soon."

As he spoke his eyes seldom left Ellen's face. She sat on the ground, glancing up at him, but mostly keeping her eyelids down. Then she said shyly, and unexpectedly, "We have plenty of provisions, Mr. Craddock. Would you consider joining us?"

Angharad shot her an indignant look and was about to speak, and Miranda, realising that she would certainly make some comment which would emphasize Huw Craddock's lower station in life, said quickly, "Yes, do stay a while. You would be doing the pony a favour as well as us. Mrs. Rhys has packed far too much for our needs, and we will only have to carry it home."

"We could leave it for the rabbits and squirrels," said Angharad sulkily.

"And so you shall, Miss Angharad," said Huw Craddock. "I eat sparingly during the day, but I will gladly take a little something with you."

Miranda glanced at Dafydd, who sat slightly apart from them drinking his ale and decided that he would be chaperon enough for a few minutes. "Come, Angharad," she cajoled, "let us pick some flowers for your Mama."

Instantly diverted, the girl rose and darted deeper into the forest to be followed more slowly by Miranda, who, having acted on impulse in leaving Ellen with her admirer, now wondered if she had been less than discreet. But then she had her faculties fully occupied in trying to prevent Angharad from climbing impossible places where the mountain over-hung the glade. "But the best flowers always seem just out of reach, Miranda," wailed Angharad. "There, look, just above our heads is a yellow woodsage. I must have it for Mama!"

She dodged Miranda and scrambled up a steep bank, sending down a shower of small stones, twigs and dank earth and perched out of reach, laughing mockingly. "You cannot follow me here, can you?"

Miranda tried to keep irritation out of her voice. "I could do so if I wished, but there is no need. Please pick your flower and come down."

"But if I do we will have to return to the others and that was not your plan, was it? It is no good, you know, Ellen will never be beguiled by a hulking farmer like Huw Craddock. But you should not worry, Miranda, and think up little ruses to take my cousin's mind from her intention. Mr. Glendower will never take Ellen, of that you may be sure."

Miranda felt cold and sick as she spoke in a voice just above a whisper. "Angharad! You are saying monstrous things. I am sure you cannot realise. Your Mama . . ."

She choked on the words, and Angharad began to scramble down the bank. "Come, Miranda, you must not be upset by my teasing."

"Is that what you call it? But it is not at all funny to say such things."

"Oh, I do not think they are funny, I assure you. Come, let us join the others."

Huw Craddock had finished his meal and rose as they approached. "I must be on my way then. Thank you, ladies, for a most delicious luncheon. I look forward to seeing you at the gathering for Mrs. Glendower's birthday —if not before."

He addressed them all, but his eyes were on Ellen, and she watched him as he mounted his pony, gave a final wave and trotted away through the forest.

Chapter Eleven

Lora's birthday fell on October the twelfth, and the bustle of preparations for the party reverberated through the house. Angharad took Ellen and Miranda to see the reception apartments usually kept closed.

The largest dated from an early time, and the mullioned windows ended in deep window seats. A raised platform at one end of the hall had once been used by the master and his family for meals with the household who sat below them in the body of the hall, and Angharad explained that now it was useful for the musicians. A Georgian Glendower had built Adam fireplaces at either end of the hall, and two of the long windows had been converted into doors, which opened onto a flagged courtyard where variegated chrysanthemums and late roses grew in tubs.

The floor was of highly polished oak. "For the dancing," said Angharad, her eyes alight with anticipation. "This year I am to be allowed to stay up quite late." She twirled to the centre of the floor and bent her knee in a graceful curtsey, almost colliding with a village woman who knelt polishing.

"There will be no holding her," muttered Ellen. "How thankful I am, Miranda, that you came to live here, otherwise I can see I might have had the sole task of trying to control my cousin."

Miranda glanced curiously at Ellen as they strolled back to the schoolroom to resume their dilatory sewing on the despised gown ordered by Mrs. Mowbray. Sometimes, of late, she had become quite dreamy and spent long minutes gazing from the window toward the distant hills. She had also taken to wandering off on walks, sometimes on the shore, more often out onto the wide estuary sands.

Miranda ventured to remonstrate with her one day. "I get worried, Ellen, when I think you may be out there. How can you be sure you will not stray where it is dangerous; or even that you will not fall into a deep pool, or be cut off by the tide?"

Ellen laughed. "I, too, felt nervous when first I came here, but one is quite safe provided all precautions are taken. Angharad is able to tell me the exact times of the tides, and for the rest I watch where I put my feet.

"Oh, Miranda, it is so lovely out there. The solitude is what I most enjoy. The wind sings across the sands and through the marsh grasses, and I feel at one with the elements and the wild creatures. I am beginning to know something of the habits of the birds."

"Well," smiled Miranda, "please remember that you are not as they are and able to fly from danger. I must confess I have quite a fear of the estuary."

"I have not! And out there, my view of the beautiful mountains is not impeded. I have grown to love them, too, Miranda."

And perhaps one who inhabits them, thought Miranda, but she could not say so aloud. Imperceptibly, the quiet girl had become dear to her, yet she still maintained a dignity and reserve that could not lightly be encroached upon.

They had almost finished their party gowns and had hidden them in dust covers in Miranda's wardrobe. Mrs. Mowbray chivied them about their slow progress on Ellen's approved dress, and they were forced to give their precious time to making up a garment which they both knew she would never wear.

Mrs. Glendower sat out of bed everyday and sometimes strolled along the upper corridors, leaning on her husband's arm. Miranda, who had been fitting and altering the black velvet gown, was touched to see how gentle he had become with the frail woman, and if pangs of jealousy surprised her at the sight of them so close she stifled them at birth. Lora had insisted that she would wear unrelieved black, but Miranda could not help protesting. "You will look charming with your white skin and auburn hair, ma'am, but would you not consider a touch of something else—white perhaps. Do say you will."

Lora hesitated. "I don't know—I don't know." Her eyes strayed as they so often did to the picture of the lovers in her room, and Miranda wondered if she saw herself in that pleading woman. And who could be the man who turned from her in anguish?

Miranda went on gently, "I have a present which I was keeping for your birthday, but it would do so very well with your gown. I would so much like to give it to you now. Please allow me to."

With Lora's reluctant permission, she tacked handmade lace cuffs on to the sleeves, which ended at the elbow and, at the neck, a collar to match. She had begun them long ago as a pleasurable exercise, but had finished them for Lora. The filmy lace fell over the sick woman's wrists, concealing their painful thinness, and her graceful neck and well-set head, rising from the foamy collar, took on a fragile beauty.

"Oh, Miranda, did you really work these for me? I shall not have a more wonderful present."

"I think you are right, my dear." They had not heard Bailey admit Mr. Glendower, and Lora turned to him. "See what Miranda has made for me, dear. I am going to wear them to my party. I think I have never owned lace so lovely."

Miranda was delighted by her enthusiasm. "If you will give me the gown, ma'am, I will sew the lace on securely."

She turned to leave, but Mr. Glendower called her back. "Miranda, you do understand that you will be attending the party—as a guest."

Miranda smiled. "Oh, yes, thank you. Mrs. Mowbray told me I was to be permitted to come. I am really looking forward to it."

Mr. Glendower's heavy brows drew together in a frown. "Permitted to come! I repeat, Miranda, you will be a guest."

"Of course you will," cried Lora. "And she shall dance the night away, shall she not, Gethin?"

Miranda could not meet his eyes, and he bowed, kissed his wife's cheek, and left. Miranda watched how Lora's gaze followed him from the room. "He is a good man, Miranda. A fine man. I have been at fault . . . at fault . . ." Her voice broke, then she continued in stronger tones. "Bailey, help me out of my gown, please, and Miss Courtney can take it away with her." The maid obeyed and handed it to Miranda with a sniff and a look of dislike.

In the corridor, Miranda paused at a window overlooking the sea, wondering how great a part Merrick and Mrs. Pritchett had in Bailey's aversion to her. She supposed that they had not spared her with their spiteful tongues. But she had done no wrong, so how could they harm her? She took a last look at the sea and saw that a heavy mist was creeping in with the tide. She carried Mrs. Glendower's gown to the schoolroom, where Gwennie had lighted a welcome fire. The mist was whirling in over the estuary and bringing with it a damp cold which seemed to penetrate the bones, but she felt cosy and protected as she sat before the dancing flames.

Gwennie brought in an oil lamp. "It's getting that dark, miss, and you don't want to wear out your eyes now, do you? It's the mist, see. It comes down that sudden it catches the fishermen out at times, though they are experts at foretelling the weather. I think that's why the master is so strict about not allowing any of us on the estuary without asking permission. He has a chart which tells the height and depth of the tide, and knows where it is safe to venture. But usually he sends us with one of the men and ponies, too."

Miranda had been paying little heed to Gwennie, who frequently chattered and seemed only to want someone sympathetic to be present. During her short and unloved existence she had never had the luxury of an uncritical audience before being lifted from the kitchen to a life of undreamed of comfort.

Miranda smiled indulgently at her before the import of the maid's words pierced her consciousness. "Did you say that Mr. Glendower allows no one out on the sands without his permission? But Miss Ellen has been walking out there quite often and without any escort. Miss Angharad has been giving her the tide times."

Gwennie was startled. "Well, I'm sure she knows. She could read them in her Da's study, I suppose. That's where he keeps the maps and charts."

"Have you seen Miss Ellen lately, Gwennie?"

"Not for an hour or so. Then she said . . ." The maid's eyes flew open, and her hand to her mouth.

Miranda leapt up so suddenly that her pins, Lora's gown, her needle cushion, scattered over the floor, "What is it, Gwennie? Where is Miss Ellen?"

". . . I don't know, miss, for sure. But she said something about a walk. I wasn't attending properly, but I think she mentioned the estuary . . . where are you going? You can't go out there!"

Without coherent thought Miranda sped through the corridors and out of the front door of Ynys Noddfa. The mist writhed and curled like a live creature as Miranda darted in and out of the cold, damp patches until she reached the edge of the sand. Only it was covered now by water which crept higher, lapping at her feet, sucking at the grasses and turning firm places into deathly traps.

"Dear God," breathed Miranda, "please don't let Ellen be out there." She called her name, but the mist caught her voice and threw it back in mocking echoes. Miranda turned and ran. She hammered wildly on the front door, which someone had closed, and it was opened by Merrick, who stared stupidly at her as she demanded, "Where is Mr. Glendower?"

He gulped. "You got no call to come in this way. He's in his study, I think, why do . . ."

Miranda burst through the study door without knocking. "What the devil? I thought I left orders I was not to be disturbed . . . Miranda! Is it you? What's the matter? Has someone upset you?"

"Ellen!" she gasped. "I think Ellen is out on the estuary sands."

He wasted no time in questions or in speculation, but grabbing her hand raced her out of the house, past the open-mouthed butler, to the stables where he shouted orders. At once, several men appeared, one leading Mr.

Glendower's big horse. He leapt onto its bare back and galloped off, leaving others to mount and follow him. Miranda seemed to have been forgotten, and in moments the stable yard was empty. She ran to the edge of the water which was higher, in time to see a rowboat swallowed up by the mist.

Muffled shouts sometimes reached her ears, and once she thought she caught the dip of oars, but mostly there was silence except for the lapping water, which forced her repeatedly to move back. She started at a touch on her arm and saw with surprise that Gwennie was there, holding out her warm cloak. She slipped it over her shoulders, realising for the first time that she was shaking with cold. She and Gwennie stood together silently. News must have travelled through the house, for they were joined by Mrs. Mowbray, whose face was paper white and whose lips were trembling. She looked old and ill, and Miranda ventured to take her arm. Mrs. Mowbray leaned heavily on her, and Miranda saw that, after all, this rigid disciplinarian truly cared for Ellen.

For what seemed an interminable time they stood, wordlessly straining to see and hear. Then came sounds; men's voices, the whinny of a pony, again the dip of oars, and as a patch of mist lifted for an instant they saw Mr. Glendower, seated in the rowboat, supporting a limp figure in his arms.

"She's drowned," moaned Mrs. Mowbray. "Oh, Ellen, my child . . ."

The boat touched the shore, and the oarsmen helped Mr. Glendower to his feet as he held fast to the still form of his cousin. "It's all right, Cousin Augusta. We reached her in time, but she is suffering from cold and shock. She will need all your mothering for a while."

Miranda helped the anxious mother to undress Ellen and massage her cold limbs before they pulled up the covers of her well-warmed bed. Ellen's teeth had stopped chattering, and she managed a wan smile and a slight grimace as Mrs. Mowbray insisted on her downing a glass of hot milk well laced with rum, before she sank into exhausted slumber.

Miranda left Mrs. Mowbray seated by her daughter's

bed, watching Ellen's face intently, and as she closed the bedroom door she leaned back on it and closed her eyes. She felt suddenly drained of strength as she realized how close Ellen had come to death.

"Are you ill?" Mr. Glendower's voice sounded close. She had not heard his approach over the thick carpeting, and she started. "Just tired," she murmured.

He took her arm and drew her along the corridor and she followed unresistingly as lassitude crept over her, eating her reserves of will. Almost without knowing it she found herself seated in Mr. Glendower's study before the fire, a glass of brandy and water in her hand. She took a sip and choked a little. "This is the second time you have revived me with strong drink, sir. I am not accustomed to spirits. My Papa . . ."

"Your Papa would not allow you to drink them and quite correctly, too. But I am sure he would consider me failing in my duty if I did not administer the treatment you so obviously need. You also are suffering from shock and, as usual, you have been thinking of others and not yourself. But now I will look after you. I would always . . ." He stopped and turned from her to stir the glowing coals with the toe of his boot. "Sip your brandy and bring some colour back to your face."

She did so and gradually the sick feeling was replaced by a comforting glow. She stared at her employer's back, her eyes travelling over the broad shoulders to the muscular legs encased in fine leather. She noted how his dark hair waved a little over his well-shaped head, and her heart lurched and almost betrayed her into crying out her love and longing for him. She knew she must go, yet her body seemed unwilling to obey her command. He raised his hands to the mantel piece and clenched his fists. Then all at once his shoulders slumped, and he swung round to look at her with an expression of hopelessness.

"To have you near me is torment, Miranda, but I keep my promise. No declarations of love, I said, and I meant it. It would be far greater misery to have you leave."

Again he fell silent before he said slowly. "I have been speaking with Angharad, and she wept and stormed her penitence at Ellen's dreadful experience, swearing so violently that she must have made a mistake in the information she gave about the tide that I was driven to the awful conclusion that she had some purpose in her lies. You see, Miranda, although I know her to be . . . slow . . . she does understand the tides. I have made a special point of instructing her, knowing that she could never be allowed to roam free, were she not so taught. I am pushed to the conclusion that she sent Ellen out onto the estuary at a time when she knew the risks. But why? That is what I keep asking myself? Why should she show such malice towards one who has offered nothing but friendship?"

"Angharad is jealous of her," said Miranda. The words were out before she considered their implication.

Mr. Glendower's eyebrows were raised. "Jealous? How can this be? Ellen has so little; no money or prospects or position. How can Angharad be jealous?"

"I don't know," lied Miranda miserably.

"Look at me! You do know and I want you to tell me. I have a right to such knowledge. This is my house; these people are my family!"

Miranda swallowed, then spoke rapidly. "Angharad fears that you will love Ellen more than you do her." Now that the subject had been broached, she determined to say what had long been in her mind. "Indeed, sir, you do seem to spurn Angharad, when it is clear that she loves you devotedly." He kept his eyes fixed on her face as she stammered on. "Angharad thinks—fears—that her mother will die—that Ellen will be set up in her place as your—wife. I suppose that Angharad does not want a stepmother. I can see no other reason for . . ."

"No, you cannot!" His harsh voice halted her. He began to pace the floor, his brows drawn together, the lines etched deeply into his face. "You cannot see reasons, but I can. I know what is in Angharad's twisted mind, and I tell you, Miranda, it is unendurable to me."

He continued to pace, speaking now so quietly that she believed he voiced his thoughts aloud. "The child should go from here, yet how to accomplish it! Her mother would never consent. And where should she go?"

Miranda watched him, feeling confused and unhappy.

She had learned that he and his wife had long since ceased to share a bedroom, but she had not known whether he had left his wife's bed because of her weakness or out of distaste for her body. He had told Miranda that he loved her, yet the emotions here seemed so tangled and inward-looking that it was impossible to tell if his interpretation of love agreed with hers.

At last he stood still and said flatly, "Please, would you go to my wife, Miranda. I know that someone will have told her by now of these ghastly events, and she looks to you for her comfort. Contrive to let her believe it was accidental."

Lora was half reclining on a chaise longue. She wore a wrapper of leaf-green silk, and her newly brushed hair hung halfway down her back. With a fire-induced flush she looked lovely, but immeasurably fragile, and Miranda felt the familiar stab of pity. Lora scarcely waited for Bailey to leave before asking, "What has Angharad done? What has happened to my child? Is Ellen recovered?"

Miranda sat down beside the agitated woman. "Ellen is well and resting. What have you heard, Mrs. Glendower?"

"Bailey told me some tale of Angharad sending Ellen out on a pretext and causing her to go to the estuary, when she knew perfectly well that Ellen would be in terrible danger. Say it isn't so, Miranda!"

Miranda patted Lora's hand. "As usual, ma'am, a story has become garbled in the telling. Of course Miss Angharad did not *send* Miss Ellen anywhere. Is it likely that a grown woman would allow herself to be ordered by a child? She mistook the tide times, and Ellen nearly became stranded. She was chilled and damp, but now she is sleeping it off."

"Oh, if I could be sure that were all!" Lora dropped Miranda's hand and rose shakily to her feet, drawing her wrapper about her and walking to the window. "I chose this side of the house because the estuary frightens me so. It always has. It keeps me prisoner you see, creeping upon me like a gaoler. I fear it in all of its moods. It waits there to trap the unwary."

She swung round, her wrapper flying out around her.

room. The platform was banked with hothouse blooms, and their sweet scents filled the air. The musicians had arrived and were setting up their stands to rehearse. Housemaids were giving a final shine to the floor, and wood and coals lay ready in the fireplaces. Then Angharad dragged Miranda to a smaller adjoining room whose windows also overlooked the walled garden. Tables had been set, and the longest already held covered dishes into which Angharad peeped with cries of excitement.

"Vol-au-vent of oysters, lobster patties, apples and melons, game pies, cheese cakes! And later there will be so much more. Pastries and fruit tarts, cream and jelly moulds—and ices—did you know we have an ice-freezing machine, Miranda? Cheeses, biscuits, wood pigeons and wild duck! Oh, it is an endless variety when we have a party.

"And Ynys Noddfa is noted also for the quality of its liquid refreshment. We shall have Claret Granito—that is one of Merrick's specialties—it is made with oranges, you know; and cold punch and fruit cup, Moselle cup and Shandy Gaff. And there will be wine, too, in our beautiful carafes. Do you not long for the evening to come, Miranda?"

"There is more to a party than eating and drinking," teased Miranda.

"Oh, yes, there is, there is. There will be dancing, and I shall dance with Mr. Glendower. You will see how well we shall look together."

Once more she twirled in imminent danger of over-setting one of the little chairs set about the smaller tables, each table adorned with a bohemian glass vase of autumn foliage and berries. They were about to leave when a perspiring Mrs. Rhys entered, giving directions to a scared-looking footman. At the sight of what he carried, both Angharad and Miranda gasped with pleasure. From a large flat dish rose a marvel of spun sugar. Delicate spirals in pastel colours spanned an archway below which was an icing sugar seat on which sat a porcelain figure of a woman, while at her feet knelt her porcelain lover, his hands forever raised in pleading.

In her agitation Mrs. Rhys spoke in Welsh to Miranda,

but her meaning was clear, and when the centre piece had been securely placed in the middle of the table, her explosive sigh of relief was echoed by all of them.

"Oh, Mrs. Rhys, did you make it? You are so clever! Only see the tiny figures. The little lady is smiling. I am sure she means to be kind to her adorer." Angharad peered so closely that Mrs. Rhys exclaimed with apprehension, and Miranda hastily took the girl's arm and led her away.

"Come, dear, it is lunch time, and then your mama has given orders that you must rest. It is of no use to argue, you must obey her. But I will come to your room and read to you if you will promise to try to sleep."

When Miranda went to Angharad's room, she found her already in bed, her beautiful hair spread over the snowy pillow. She held a book. "Cousin Augusta has begun to fill my shelves with uplifting literature, as she calls it, which she says must be read to me, but I wish you would read from Hans Christian Andersen. You do not think his works unfitting for me, do you Miranda?"

"Certainly not," replied Miranda firmly. "My own dear Mama read to me often from his story and poetry books. Which is your favourite?"

"The Ugly Duckling," replied Angharad at once. "The poor little duck makes me think of myself and how I shall grow into a lovely swan and triumph over my enemies."

"But you are not ugly, and what enemies have you?"

"No, I think I am not ugly, Miranda, but there are those who will be amazed when I come into my own."

She gave her secretive smile, and Miranda sighed. She never would understand the girl. She began to read in quiet tones, and Angharad listened with unusual patience, her satisfaction with the story's ending showing in her face. Then, at her insistence, Miranda sang to her some of the melodies she had heard from her own mother until Angharad's heavy lids drooped over the large eyes and she slept.

For a moment Miranda stood gazing at the sleeping girl, who looked so young and innocent and quite incapable of wicked mischief. Yet she was no child! She was almost a woman and seemed, at times, to know a woman's dreams and longings, and Miranda shivered in sudden fear, before she tiptoed from the room.

Chapter Twelve

The family ate an early light meal that evening and dispersed to dress for the party. Ellen crept in her wrapper to Miranda's room to finish her toilette, and Gwennie jigged about in her excitement as she helped the two girls.

Miranda's dress was cut in a princess style with the blue-green brocade forming an apron front ending at her knees with two bows of the same material. The grey ribbed silk was bordered at her feet with blue-green accordion pleating and looped with more bows of the same colour at the sides, and the low neck was edged with lace, which also graced the elbow-length sleeves. She wore her mother's simple pearl necklace and ear-drops and pinned up her hair with flowers she had fashioned from remnants of the brocade.

Gwennie clasped her hands in delight as she stared at her, then both turned to help Ellen. As Miranda had expected, the dark-blue damask with the shining silver threads was exactly the foil Ellen needed to her pale, but perfect, skin. Miranda had cut the gown in a severe style, knowing that anything fussy would overwhelm Ellen's delicate colouring, and her figure looked appealing in its slenderness. They rejected the amber beads advised by Mrs. Mowbray, and Ellen produced a charming sapphire and silver necklace and ear-drops, which had been a present from her Papa in their richer days.

Then, ignoring Ellen's half-laughing protests, Miranda sat her down and brushed her hair, coiling the silver strands into loops over her small ears, completing her task with a spray of silver flowers with dark-blue velvet leaves. The girls smoothed on their white elbow length gloves and picked up their fans; Miranda's of peacock feathers and Ellen's of Nottingham lace, before they stood in front of the cheval glass and surveyed themselves and each other with mutual satisfaction.

Ellen's eyes were glowing. She looks like a woman about to meet her lover, thought Miranda, but that must be impossible. So far as she knew Ellen had met no man except Mr. Craddock since arriving at Ynys Noddfa, and surely she could not be so lost to reality as to view him with any particularity.

Miranda knew that she herself had never looked better. Gethin Glendower would see her as the woman she was meant to be and not a seamstress in drab. The thought came swiftly enough to slip under her guard, and she flushed. Well, perhaps there could be no harm in enjoying the admiration in his eyes. Soon she must complete plans to leave the island before she became hopelessly tangled in illicit hopes and dreams.

"It is almost seven. The guests will be arriving. It seems strange to think of them leaving their carriages and coming across the sands on ponies dressed in all their finery."

"Not so to them, perhaps," said Miranda. "I think they must all be used to riding. The country here is so mountainous that they cannot always use vehicles. Angharad says it is quite a sight to see the line of ponies crossing the estuary, each led by a man carrying a lantern, while the moon shines on the scene. She said it was like a cavalcade from one of her story books."

Ellen laughed gaily. "I do not think I have ever looked forward more to an evening. I promised to visit Cousin Lora before going downstairs. She suggested that you might like to come with me."

Lora looked alarmingly fragile as she stood in her black velvet, while Bailey helped her to smooth on her gloves, but she smiled at them warmly. "Am I not grand?" And see what my husband has given me for my birthday." She gestured towards a magnificent brooch of diamonds and gold set at her breast. "And thank you, Ellen, for your gift." She picked up a fan of appliqued black lace. "Angharad's present was these gloves of such soft kid they have almost a velvet touch. And your Mama, Ellen, brought me this.' She pointed to the bed, where lay a jacket of seal fur. "I am so grateful to you all for making my birthday such a happy one. And you see, Miranda, you were quite right when you said that your enchanting lace would enhance my gown."

She spoke of happiness, but her eyes were bleak and her speech too rapid. Her smiles never reached her eyes, and Miranda felt cold at the misery she sensed beneath the brittle surface. Lora went to her dressing table, and as she talked extracted something from a small gold case. "I asked everyone to meet me in my room before going down. I don't really know why. A sick woman's whim perhaps. This may be the last time that we . . ." She stopped and Ellen's eyes met Miranda's briefly before she said, "You must not have morbid thoughts today, Cousin Lora. You have been so much better of late. I know that you will continue to improve . . ."

She was interrupted as the door burst open, and Angharad danced into the room, her cheeks crimson with excitement. Her hair was drawn up behind with a band of pearls and satin daisies, and she looked more adult than Miranda had ever seen her. "How slow you all are! I have been ready these ten minutes. Where is Mr. Glendower?"

Lora looked closely at her daughter before drawing her near and kissing her. "How lovely you are, my darling. But you must be calmer or you will make yourself ill. Papa will be here directly. We must await him and Cousin Augusta."

Angharad grabbed her mother's arm, and Miranda saw what it was that Lora had fetched from her dressing table. Over her right glove she wore a bracelet of plaited light-brown hair fastened with a small gold clasp. "What is it, Mama? A bracelet! I have never seen it before. Whose hair is it? Oh, is it *his* . . . oh, Mama, how romantic . . ."

"Angharad . . ." Lora's voice was weak and she looked ready to faint.

Miranda took a step towards her, but was stopped by a voice from the door. "I see we are ready. How very charming a picture you make, ladies."

by Ellen and a man unknown to Miranda. "He's a widower," whispered Angharad. "My Cousin Augusta would be glad if he should offer for Ellen. I think she must have quite given up hope of Ellen taking my Mama's place here."

Miranda glanced around. "Angharad! You must not say such things—especially here. Indeed, you must not even think them."

"Oh, I do not, I assure you. Ellen stands no chance with Mr. Glendower. One day you'll all see. Look at poor Mama. She has to sit already. She is quite feeble, is she not? Only one turn about the room, and she looks ready to drop."

Miranda hurried to Lora's side. "My dear ma'am, is there anything I can do for you?"

"Thank you, my dear, but my husband has gone to procure me a little wine. My strength is not yet returned."

"But you are so much improved. It can only be a matter of time."

"I think not, Miranda. I think not . . ." She pressed a handkerchief to her lips and began to twist the hair bracelet. Then Mr. Glendower returned and, with a courtly bow, handed his wife a glass. "Sherry, Lora, my dear. It will give you courage."

Miranda was startled. Why had he used that word? Surely he had meant to say strength. Lora was sipping the wine, gazing up at her husband with an expression of such anguish that instinctively Miranda moved herself between her and the guests. A little colour stole back into Lora's face, and she smiled tremulously. "Take Miranda onto the floor, Gethin. Then you must introduce her to some gentlemen. She must not waste her beauty in tending me."

He held out his arm, and Miranda placed her fingertips on it. They faced one another as the musicians struck a chord. He bowed; she curtseyed, then she was in his arms, whirling to the rhythm of a waltz. Round they danced, and she felt all the mingled emotions which had betrayed her in the past weeks being fused into a love and longing so intense that she could scarcely find breath. He said not a word until, as the dance ended, he bowed once more

175

outraged countenance
re would be no chance
ie young farmer was

olding Angharad. She
ed to be in an ecstatic
:id shoes kept perfect
looking down on her
seemed to show when
i, and again Miranda
pted him to reject his

her to other men, and
compliments, but al-
proper responses, she
Glendower to ask her
vould not. Maybe he
oyee twice in one eve-

had spent the evening
eiving her guests' con-
talking of retiring. "I
was explaining to yet
e not been downstairs
know that my guests
and that their enjoy-
you cannot any of you
laughed, but her voice

stab of joy that Gethin Glendower was asking her for another dance. Again she was filled with happiness, and this time he did speak. "I have not told you, Miranda, how very beautiful I find you tonight. I know you are always lovely; even Cousin Augusta's drab gowns cannot hide it, but tonight you are a goddess . . . a witch . . . who would break down all my defences and destroy all my resolve."

"Mr. Glendower, you must not!"

"For God's sake, Miranda, let there be an end to such formality between us—at least for tonight. I am Gethin to you, as you are Miranda to me, and have been since I kissed you on the shore, have I not? My lovely, tempestuous Miranda . . ."

"Please, don't! Someone will hear you."

"Let them. Let them all hear me."

She glanced at him in alarm and realised that he had drunk more than had seemed obvious. Usually he drank sparingly, but extra toasts taken with his guests had clearly had their effect. They had reached one of the garden doors, opened wide to allow some air, for the evening had turned unseasonably close, and she stopped dancing and fanned herself, saying in a deliberately affected voice for the benefit of other ears, "I think I will walk outside. Pray permit me to leave you, Mr. Glendower. You will not miss me. There are many ladies who have claims upon their host."

For a moment his eyebrows were raised, then he seized her elbow and almost lifted her into the flagged garden, where they stood in a flood of moonlight. Out here there was a small breeze, and after the overheated atmosphere of the ballroom, it made her shiver in her thin silk gown.

"You little fool," exclaimed Gethin. "You'll catch your death!"

He slipped out of his jacket, threw it around her shoulders ignoring her protest, and led her to the shadow of the high wall. She stood quite still, the body warmth from his coat seeping into her. She must return to the ballroom—she must!

"Miranda . . .!"

"Let me go, please. I have to go back. Please don't obstruct my way—please . . ."

"Miranda, I love you!"

"You promised, oh, you promised!"

"I have kept my word, but I am human. And if you could see yourself as I do. If you could see your loveliness in there—and here in the moonlight. Other men have held you tonight. Other men have looked on you and desired you—and some of them have the right to want you. They are free and could offer the protection of their names in honour. But I cannot and I would give my soul if I could."

He stared hard at her then said roughly, "Why do you not answer me, Miranda? I apologise for breaking my promise, though I don't see why I should when I cannot be really sorry. I love you so much my life is a daily agony to me. But I will keep myself in order, that I swear, if you will only forgive my speaking to you tonight. It is more than a man can bear to see you and not to hold you, loving you as I do."

"You can't—I won't allow it!"

"My God, but you are cruel! Is this to be my punishment for being human? Am I to be left without comfort of any sort because I spoke to you of love?"

"I would not punish you. I had already decided before this evening. I can't stay, truly I cannot, because I . . ."

"Yes? Because you what?"

"Lora is your wife."

"You have known that from the beginning and that is *not* what you began to say!"

He took both her hands in his and drew her close. She couldn't struggle. Another couple had entered the garden and was strolling beneath the moon. She heard a woman's light laugh carried on the clear air.

"Let me go," she whispered.

"Not until you have told me what you were about to say! You cannot stay because . . . were you going to say 'I love you?' Is that it?"

Pushed beyond her limits Miranda said in strangled tones, "Yes, it is. And now that you have forced me to

178

make an admission which shames me, perhaps you are satisfied."

He pulled her closer to him. "Don't be ashamed, my little one. You have done no wrong. In taking my love you take nothing that is valued in this house."

"But Lora . . ."

"Lora does not love me. But I love you and you admit that you return my love. Oh, Miranda, fy nghalon i, my heart!"

He released her hands abruptly, and his arms were around her. Blindly, unthinkingly, she looked up at him and his lips were on hers. She pushed at him, but he was immovable in his muscular strength, and then, as his lips wandered softly over hers, over her cheeks, her chin, and back to her mouth, she found her arms stealing, it seemed, of their own volition about his neck. His jacket fell from her shoulders as his mouth became hot and demanding, and for breathless seconds she returned a kiss of such passion it left her shaking.

"Yes, my little Miranda, you do love me. I know now that you do, and there will be no more talk of leaving me, eh?"

"Gethin, I . . ."

"Oh, it is good to hear you say my name at last. So many years without love and now you, my darling. It was worth the waiting."

"Gethin, you cannot be suggesting that I stay here and that we conduct an illicit affair beneath this roof."

"Of course not. I am not so lost to honour! For a time we will simply enjoy the knowledge of one another's presence, as do all lovers, and later you will find a good reason for leaving, and I will make a home for us."

"You mean you will take me for a mistress!"

He put his hand over her lips. "Don't desecrate our love, darling. To me you will be a wife as no other woman has, or ever could. I will continue to do my duty here as landowner—so many depend on me—but I will do it with such joy, knowing that you will be awaiting me somewhere."

"No, Gethin, I shall not. There is no use in arguing with me. I am determined to leave your house as soon

179

as possible, tomorrow I daresay, and I shall endeavour not to see you again. You are tied to Lora, and already our love is besmirched by what has taken place between us. Do not destroy my self-respect forever."

At these words his protests died, and he stared down at her. She could not read his face, which was in shadow, but she felt his pain. When finally he spoke he said in low tones, "Miranda, where would you go? What would you do? The world is a cold and cruel place to those who have been tenderly reared and are without means."

She shivered again, not this time from cold, but from the memory of the bleak servant's hostel and the poor little governess. "I . . . I have no clear plan, as yet, but there must be a place for someone who is skilled with her needle. I will find somewhere."

"If you are determined, my darling, then allow me to help you. I have many friends, both here and in England. I can write to them . . ."

Her heart was pounding in her efforts to control her ravaged feelings. "That would mean you would know where I was! No, it will not do. I must make my own way, and if you love me truly you will not tempt me further, indeed, you must not."

Her control broke and a sob escaped her. He grasped her hands. "I cannot let you go, Miranda. I will not let you! I have waited all my life for you and I mean to keep you. Do not try my patience too far. I am not one of your easy men to give way before fine words and noble phrases when I know that below them lies a love of which I have dreamed. I have a passionate nature which has long been in check, but now I have found a woman I love—and who loves me. Oh, Miranda you do love me. You would not lie. Say you will stay or that you will wait for me somewhere."

His voice had risen, and she looked around distractedly, "Oh, hush, someone will hear you. Your wife trusts me —I cannot deceive her. And I cannot be led into such a position as you describe, Gethin, it would degrade our love."

"There is no power on earth that could do that! But perhaps you are thinking of a higher power—remember-

180

ing Papa's teachings, no doubt!"

At Miranda's small cry of protest at his scorn he murmured, "Forgive me, dearest, that was unworthy. It is only that I am so desperate!"

His voice cracked on the last word, and Miranda feared that if she heard more she would weaken. She loved him so much that it was torture to run from him, but she did. Picking up her skirts, she fled across the flagged courtyard, and the couple still strolling in the garden looked up startled. The man was Huw Craddock, and the girl holding tightly to his arm had hair which gleamed like quicksilver in the moonlight. Even in the midst of her confusion Miranda wondered how Ellen had escaped her mother's vigilance for so long.

She stopped briefly at the garden door to smooth her hair and compose herself as best she could. The first person she saw as she entered the ballroom was Mrs. Mowbray, who grasped her roughly by the arm. "Have you seen Miss Ellen? Is she in the garden with *that man?* I daresay she is and you know it! And do not suppose that your departure with Mr. Glendower went unnoticed by me. I shall have something to say to you later!"

She stalked out into the night and returned flanked by a flushed Ellen and an angry-looking Huw Craddock. Miranda was on the point of deciding to take refuge in her room when Bailey appeared. "Mrs. Glendower wishes you to attend her. She says she is weary and would like your company." Her eyes spoke all the angry jealousy she felt.

Lora was very pale and her eyes were ringed by deep shadows. "Ah, Miranda, my dear, I have made my apologies and farewells to my guests and think I will retire. I would so like to talk with you a while, if you would be so kind."

Miranda's throat felt tight. Lora's voice was supplicating and she felt sharp guilt. Did Lora suspect that her husband desired her seamstress? But surely she would not speak to her with such affection if she did.

Miranda put her strong young arm about Lora, who was trembling now in an effort to walk. She staggered and recovered herself as they were joined by Gethin, who supported his wife from the other side. In this way they left the ballroom, Lora still smiling with great sweetness at her guests. As they passed the supper room, Miranda saw Mrs. Pritchett and Merrick, who had their heads close together as they stared at the passing group. In the faces of the servants were scorn and derision which seared Miranda to the soul and which she felt she must deserve.

The windows of the supper room were also opened onto the garden, and she guessed that she and Gethin had been seen together and that perhaps part of her conversation with him had been overheard. There could be no more room for doubt as to her future. Tomorrow she would rise early and enlist Dafydd's help in leaving.

Gethin kissed his wife's brow and wished her a good night, and Bailey and Miranda helped her to bed. Lora thanked her maid before she dismissed her and asked Miranda to sit with her a little. "I know it is selfish of me, dear, when there is so much gaiety downstairs. Your feet must be itching to join the dancers. I know mine used to be. Well, I will not keep you long. Tonight I need to talk to someone and you, dearest Miranda, seem almost like the sister I never had. How I wish we had met earlier, though to be sure you would have been too young for me. But if I had had a confidante like you perhaps I would not have allowed my troubles to overcome me. Or perhaps I was lost the moment I agreed to marry Gethin."

Miranda felt the sick woman's words enter her consciousness like darts, but now her head jerked at the implications of Lora's flat statement.

"Dear ma'am, you must not say these things to me. It is not fitting. Tomorrow you will regret . . ."

Lora raised her hand in an unexpectedly imperious gesture. "Be silent, my dear. Tonight I will talk, then never again."

Belying her own words she fell silent for several minutes, and again her eyes strayed to the picture of the lovers. She began to speak as if in a dream. "That picture is a cheap print, you know, but it so expresses my feelings. I insisted on having it. I think Gethin always knew why. The man who looks so desperately

182

searching . . . I see in him the lover I lost. Oh, Miranda, I have been so weak, so wretchedly foolish. Whatever happens to you, my dear, never betray your love. Never try to settle for second best. It does not do."

Miranda felt the darts twist within her. Any other man must come second to Gethin. So must she never marry?

Lora spoke again. "I once loved a man named Ifan. No, that is not quite true—I love him now—I always will, though he has been dead these many months. I think it was the knowledge of this which drove me to this illness which is killing me—this weight of sorrow and self-reproach. My old nurse sent word that Ifan was not expected to live, and I went to see him in the . . . the place where he was held.

"I went to the room in which he passed his days and tried to hold him in my arms, but he did not know me. Such hell to love and to gain no response!

"*I* sent him mad, you know, by my betrayal of our love. They told me we could not wed because of the taint of . . . of insanity which has long run through his family, but I believe he might have remained well, perhaps for years, if I had stayed true to my principles. We could have had happy years together, and I would have nursed him had he become—sick. They told me that he was violent at times and a danger, but he would not have harmed me, I know he would not."

Miranda was appalled. Tomorrow Lora would hate herself for revealing secrets which should remain locked inside her. She put out a hand and tried to speak, but Lora continued inexorably.

"We loved, Miranda. We pledged our love in the place by the lake where you picnicked, but when we wanted to legalise our union, my parents refused to give their consent. And then I heard that Ifan had been taken away and locked in *that place*. They told me that he had forgotten everyone he knew—even me whom he loved.

"When I discovered that they had lied to me, it was too late. I was married to Gethin. I wronged Ifan and I wronged Gethin and I ended with nothing but misery.

"Gethin did not join in the scheme to deceive me, never think that. He had loved me for a long time and was told that I consented to our marriage—which I did because . . . because I was forced into it. My parents hid the truth from me—they lied to me!"

Again she fell silent, and Miranda felt icy cold in spite of the fire in the grate. Gethin had been treated with abominable heartlessness by people he trusted. She asked through stiff lips, "When did your husband discover that you did not love him?"

The question brought the tears trickling down Lora's face. "When Angharad was born, I asked Gethin to take me to see Ifan. We were distant cousins, you see; friends, as well as lovers, and it seemed natural for me to visit him.

"I found my poor darling locked away from contact with the world. At first they would not let me in, but it was Gethin who insisted. We entered Ifan's room together, and when my beloved saw me he began to shout. He berated me for my faithlessness, and it was then I knew that my parents had lied. I forgot everything in my desire to explain the truth. I flung myself into his arms and told him over and over how I loved him, worshipped him until, in the end, I saw that he believed me. I had forgotten Gethin until I turned and saw his stricken look."

"Oh poor man—poor man," cried Miranda, "and what inhuman cruelty on the part of your parents. Why should they have parted you? Was there really nothing wrong with Ifan?"

Lora said flatly, "I could not say with truth that he was well. His mind held the family taint of madness, but I did not care—I adored him. Yet perhaps he was more advanced towards the darkness than I knew—maybe there was good reason for restraining him. I shall never know —and that is what tortures me most—because my visit sent him—drove him—over the razor edge of sanity into complete madness, and he truly did forget me then. I think he could not bear to remember what might have been.

"I have never been strong since that day, Miranda. And when I saw him dying, I think it sealed my own fate. I have no wish to go on without him. Knowing he was

184

in the world with me, even though he was mad, was consolation to me. But he knew me—right at the end!"

"What!" Miranda was startled. "He recognised you?"

"Just before he died, it seemed as if the cloud obscuring his mind was cleared away. He looked at me with the old loving expression and held up his arms to me. He said my name, whispered his love for me. And then he died."

Miranda felt that she would sink beneath the pall of misery generated in this room. No wonder Lora's health was ruined.

Lora spoke again. "It was the final shock that made me commit my worst folly. I returned from that place feeling as if my head would burst and destroy me. Angharad was waiting for me in my room. I paced up and down, heedless of her presence, forgetting she was only a child, and I spoke aloud all that had passed. She listened, I remember, in utter silence, then she wept and stormed, and no one could console her."

"It is to her credit that she felt such sorrow for you," said Miranda gently.

Lora turned startled eyes upon her. "She did not weep for me, but for herself."

"But why? How can a sad affair concerning you have affected her so deeply save in a sympathetic way."

"Because, in such an abrupt and cruel way, she discovered the truth about herself." Lora grasped Miranda's hand. "I . . . I have not told you all. I think you may regard me with revulsion, but I must speak. I must make you understand how greatly my darling child needs you. When I said I pledged my love for Ifan, I meant that I gave him all that a woman can give the man she loves. I loved him so and assumed we would be married. I had not expected my parents to oppose me and then . . . then . . . I found that I was with child—Ifan's child. That is why they married me to Gethin. That is how great a wrong I did him.

"He believed the baby to be his. He thought she had been born early, but even after our visit to Ifan and he discovered my deception, he continued to treat Angharad as his daughter. He is a truly great and noble man, Miranda, who deserves a better life than I have given him. When he knew about my lover he would not share a bed with me, but left me in peace. Not in any spirit of recrimination, but because he could not bear to take a woman who might find him unacceptable. And Angharad believed him to be her father until I revealed the truth to her."

Miranda could find no words and Lora, too, was silent for a while. Then she said softly, "Now you see why Angharad needs you so much, Miranda. Her governesses have left because they could not control her; or because she took a hate for them; but she loves you, I see it in the way she looks at you, in the way she continually talks of you."

Lora's thin hand went out to grasp Miranda's with surprising strength. "Promise me, Miranda, that you will not desert my little Angharad. Promise me that you will guard her at least until she is grown to be a woman."

Miranda felt sick and shaken. How could she fail to make a vow to the poor desperate creature after what had just been said? Yet how could she remain, fearing that her love for Lora's husband might destroy her powers of resistance to him? She looked into Lora's anguished eyes, which had already witnessed more suffering than anyone should be called upon to endure. Perhaps she would be given strength for the sake of the pitiful weak people who needed her.

"I will stay with Angharad," she promised in a voice she strove to keep steady.

Lora gave her no time to say more, but kissed Mirinda's hand with lips grown hot and dry. "Thank you, my dear. I thank you with all my heart."

Then she sank back on her pillows looking so white that Miranda was afraid. "Shall I call Bailey, ma'am, or Mr. Glendower?"

"No, thank you, dearest, Miranda, all will be well now that I have your promise."

Miranda stood for a moment looking down at Lora before she quietly left her side. She took one final look before leaving the room and again was irresistibly reminded of some ancient burial chamber where the deceased was surrounded by all her earthly wealth. Then she left.

Chapter Thirteen

Miranda felt too agitated to return at once to the ballroom. She sat in her room, gazing out over the moonlit
sea, and thought about Lora's revelations. They threw
light on much of Angharad's strange behaviour, yet still
did not explain Gethin's curious reluctance to display
his affection for the child, since his apparent revulsion
had begun only a short time ago and not when he discovered the trick which had been played upon him.

She started at a slight tap on her door and called,
"Enter!" Then she rose to her feet in alarm as Gethin
appeared and closed the door behind him.

"What the devil are you doing here?" he rasped. "I
expected you back long ago. Lora tells me you have
returned to the dancing, but I have been searching yet
again and could not find you. Do you feel our celebration
too much to be borne?"

She flushed at his tone. "I think there is no need for
you to speak so to me, sir."

"Sir! What foolishness is this? Come back to the ballroom, Miranda! I wish to dance with you."

"I think you have been indulging in too much wine.
I think it better if I remain here until the guests have
left. You may do or say something in public which you
will certainly regret tomorrow.

"Tomorrow! What of tomorrow? Tonight is the thing!
Eat drink and be merry, for tomorrow we may die!"

"Gethin, I beg of you, I have endured enough for
one evening."

"Ah, is the awareness of my passion so great a trial
to you? Has your love grown cold, Miranda?"

188

She tried to speak, but her voice emerged as a gasp, and when he next spoke he was calmer. "I do not behave well towards you, my darling, yet there was a time, believe it or not, when I was a gentle, sensitive boy who regarded women as saints. But I was undeceived. How I was undeceived! My wife's mother, whom I had revered as I did my own, and . . . and . . ."

"'Lora?" finished Miranda softly.

"Lora! What do you know, Miranda?"

She told him what had just been revealed to her, and he groaned. "You must take me for a fool. Cuckolded by my wife, who was aided by her unscrupulous parents. They almost ruined themselves to pay Ifan's indifferent guardian to have him put away. I must have been the greenest boy who ever lived! And that old witch of a nanny of hers *blamed* me for marrying Lora, though I did so in love and innocence. I had to send her away in the end. Her hatred made life intolerable, and she encouraged Angharad to defy me.

"And Angharad! The poor little lamb whom I adored as my own. I could not stop caring for her when I learned the truth. One cannot turn love off and on at will."

"Then why . . .?"

"Why do I repulse her? Cannot you guess? No, you are as innocent as once I was. The child had an agonising struggle to assimilate the fact that I was not the father she loved, and somewhere in her poor hazy mind her affections became distorted. She could not stop loving me, yet I was not 'Papa' any more. So I have had to comprehend that now she views me as a woman might look upon a man. I am married to her mother, but not of her blood so she sees nothing distasteful in this. But to me she will always be as a daughter."

"So that is why you show her no warmth," breathed Miranda.

"To be sure it is. It pains me to see the hurt in her face when I turn from her overtures of love, but for her own protection I must be hard on her. Poor simple child—she needs love so much—and I must not offer it to her. You, Miranda, have so much to give her. She trusts you. If only you could stay!"

He suddenly took quick strides to her and stood by her side at the window, staring into her face. "God, but you're beautiful! The moon shines for me with greater radiance when I look at you. You have said that you will leave me, so I shall consider myself absolved from my promise not to speak to you of love—just for tonight."

"But I . . ."

Her intention to tell him of her pledge to Lora was lost as he dragged her roughly into his arms and brought his lips down on hers with such fierce desire that she shuddered. But she held herself rigid and would not respond.

"Has your love grown cold, Miranda? You are going anyway, so why should I not take you here and now? No one would hear your cries for help. Tomorrow you will be gone, and I will be left only with memories, but they could hold knowledge of your tantalising, exquisite body."

She was shaking within the circle of his arms, and he let them fall to his sides. "My God, Miranda, but I'm sorry. Forgive me. I am a brute. But I love you so much. If you cared so for me you could not desert me!"

Miranda had known, even as she made her promise to Lora, that she would regret it, but now she must keep it, at least until Angharad could be found a companion whom she trusted. She would tell Gethin what had been decided, and perhaps he would grow calmer.

"I did not tell you all that was said in Lora's room, Gethin. I promised her . . ."

Again she was interrupted. This time by a light knock on her door which was opened immediately. Both turned to see Mrs. Pritchett, holding above her head a lamp which clearly illumined the scene, and caught the suspicious gleam in her small eyes. Her voice was silky as she said, "I beg your pardon, sir, I did not know you were here."

"Is it your custom to enter rooms without waiting to be called?"

"No, indeed, sir, but I believed Miss Courtney to be alone, and I was so agitated I did not think properly. You see, Miss Angharad is becoming that excited there's no doing anything with her, and Mrs. Mowbray said to bring Miss Courtney quick like, so I forgot my manners. I beg your pardon, sir—and miss."

She dropped a curtsey as Gethin stood back for Miranda to walk before him. She felt so agitated that she was sure Mrs. Pritchett must hear the thudding of her heart. The housekeeper could scarcely control the triumphant scorn which twisted her tight mouth, and Miranda knew the story of how the master was found in her bedroom in the dark would soon be all over Ynys Noddfa, no doubt with lurid embellishments.

Angharad greeted Miranda with shrill cries of joy. Her face was flushed and drops of perspiration beaded her high white brow. "Where have you been? I wanted to have more supper with you, but I was so hungry I could not wait. And I have drunk two glasses of Claret Granito, well, almost two. My stuffy Cousin Ellen came upon me and took away the glass before I had finished the second. She is altogether too pushing for my taste. She made me drink lemonade—to counteract the wine she said—but I feel so delightfully light and airy. I could dance all night long. Where is Mr. Glendower? He said he would take me on the floor again!"

"Hush, Angharad," murmured Miranda, "you are over-excited. You will be ill if you do not calm yourself. Will you walk with me in the garden for a while. I will send for wraps. The moon is almost as bright as day. It is so lovely out there."

"Why have you been out, Miranda? All by yourself? Or have you been walking with a gentleman? A lover? Miranda, I declare you are blushing. Who was he? Oh, pray do tell me."

Miranda glanced around despairingly. Several people were looking their way with amusement or disapproval. "Angharad, my dear child, you must not . . ."

But the girl danced out of her reach and began to chant, "Miranda has a lover, a lover, a lover . . ."

Merrick passed, carrying a tray of iced lemonade, and showed by the look he gave that Mrs. Pritchett had continued her work of destroying her character. She felt she could endure no more. Angharad was still twirling out of her reach and to try to catch her could lead to a scene even more humiliating. "Catch me, Miranda, if you can. I can run as fast as the wind. I can dance like a moonbeam . . ."

"Angharad!" Gethin's voice cut across the music and laughter like a sword, and instantly Angharad's face became solemn and the tripping feet were stilled. "Come here, child!"

She walked to him, dragging her pumps along the floor and stood looking down at her twisting hands. "I think Angharad, that it is time for you to retire."

"Oh, no, please do not send me away!"

"It is past midnight, and you are still a young girl. But I have not forgotten my promise. Come, my child, let us dance together."

Her face transfigured by one of her instant changes of mood, Angharad went into his arms and was whirled away among the dancers. Miranda wandered disconsolately into the supper room and sat on a little chair, pretending to nibble a biscuit. After tonight what would her life be? By now she could not doubt that even little Gwennie had heard the story of how the master and that stuck up Miss Courtney had been discovered in a compromising situation. It surprised her to discover how much she cared for Gwennie's good opinion. Perhaps because the little scullery maid represented innocence to her, she needed her devotion and trust. And when Bailey heard, how long would it be before it reached Lora's ears? How could she endure to have that poor sick woman believe that the girl she depended upon was guilty of trying to tempt her husband from her?

She suffered through the remainder of the party, dancing sometimes with men whose faces were anonymous blurs and once more with Gethin.

She had been reluctant. "Please, don't," she had begged. "The servants must all be gossiping. Let us not make matters worse."

But he had stood inexorably holding out his arms and to refuse further would be to cause more talk. They had danced for several moments before she dared to look up into his grim face, when he said, "I had to talk to you, Miranda, to apologise to you. I behaved like a

192

damned fool! Whatever possessed me to visit you in your room? But how could I know that that evil-minded housekeeper would burst in? She will have to go—and the sooner the better."

"No, Gethin. If you dismiss her it will add fuel to the scandalmonger's fires."

"What matter? You will be gone away!"

His voice was so desolate that Miranda longed to tell him of her decision to remain, but many eyes were upon them, and she did not dare risk a revelation of his feelings in so public a place. Later would do. At the end of the dance he left her with a stiff bow and when the last guest had departed over the sea-washed estuary sands, she felt almost too weary to crawl upstairs to bed, where she fell into an exhausted sleep.

In what seemed moments she was awakened by a violent shaking. "What . . .? What is it?" She sat up, pushing her tumbled hair from her face.

Gwennie was tugging at her nightgown and was babbling something in Welsh, and Miranda stared at her. The maid's face was grey, and her eyes were enormous with what looked like fear. Recovering her senses a little she spoke in English. "Oh, Miss Courtney, it's the mistress! She . . . she's dead!"

"What?" Miranda was fully awake now. "What do you mean? Mrs. Glendower? Has she been ill? Why was I not called? Oh, I can't believe it, Gwennie. You must be mistaken. That poor lady . . ."

"There's no mistake, miss, more's the pity. And no one seems to know what happened exactly. I was in the kitchen early, and Miss Bailey ordered me to carry coals to Mrs. Glendower's room."

"Yes," cried Miranda, "but what has happened?" As she spoke she swung herself out of bed, tore off her nightgown and began rapidly to dress and tidy her hair.

"Well, miss, I was close behind Bailey when we went into Mrs. Glendower's room, and Bailey drew the curtains and I looked at the bed, and the mistress was lying there looking so peaceful. I thought she was fast asleep, but then Bailey went to call her and she didn't move, and Bailey let out a screech that turned my blood, it did, and then she started in to sob over Mrs. Glendower, and then she shouted things about . . ."

Miranda kept her voice calm though she shivered with apprehension. "What things, Gwennie? What did she shout?"

"Horrible things about . . . about the master and you, miss. And she said that Mrs. Glendower was perfectly well when she retired—only tired, see, from the party, and that she for one was going to tell the doctor some of the things she knew and . . ."

"That will do, Gwennie!" Miranda tried to appear serene before Gwenne's staring eyes. Surely there was no need for the girl to look at her that way, and to be so frightened, but she remembered that she was still a child, and she put out her hand. "Come here, my dear. Don't be scared. Death is not something horrible, but only a sleep, and Mrs. Glendower seemed not to care very much for life."

"No, miss." Gwennie's hand was icy cold, and she trembled. Miranda dropped her hand sharply. Did she believe the gossip she had heard? Did she suspect her master and Miranda of—what?

But Gwennie snatched her hand back and pressed it to her lips. "I know you couldn't do no wrong, miss, no matter what they say." Then she ran out of the room, leaving Miranda to make her way slowly to Ellen's bedroom. She needed information and Ellen seemed her only friend here, since she dared not approach Gethin at present. But Ellen was not in her room, which was even neater than usual, the bed smooth and the curtains blowing in the cool October freeze.

She was about to leave when Mrs. Mowbray appeared in the doorway. She looked ill and older than her years. "You will have heard the dreadful news," she rasped. Then her lips trembled. "Such a shocking thing and as if there were not trouble enough I have to bear this." She held out a shaking hand in which she grasped a crumpled note. "I suppose you have been a party to their plan all along. It was a bad day when I engaged you to come to Ynys Noddfa!"

Miranda was bewildered. "Plan? What plan?"

194

"Read it!" commanded Mrs. Mowbray, and she thrust the note at Miranda, "though I do not doubt you are already aware of its contents."

Ellen's careful sloping writing filled the page. "My dearest Mama, I deeply regret that I feel obliged to behave in so clandestine a manner, but I knew that you would never regard my darling Huw as a suitable husband for me, so I have gone away with him. We have made and rejected so many plans during our meetings . . .'

"They have been meeting," said Miranda, raising wondering eyes to Mrs. Mowbray.

"Don't play the innocent with me, miss. You cannot deny that you have been abetting my daughter in her wickedness. Solitary walks indeed! While you have been keeping Miss Angharad out of the way!"

Miranda shook her head helplessly and read on: ". . . during our meetings, but last night when Huw and I danced together for the first time, when he held me in his arms, we both knew, that we had no choice but to spend our lives together. Huw's sister is to be my chaperon until our marriage, so have no fears, dearest Mama, that I shall disgrace your teachings, and in a few short days I shall be wed. Do not search for us. We shall not be at the farm. Please forgive me, for I could not endure to be cast out from your affections. Your most loving daughter, Ellen."

Mrs. Mowbray snatched the letter back as Miranda looked up, and began to pace the room, her silk skirts setting up a rustling like wind-lashed trees. She repeated phrases from the letter, snapping them out with fury. "Ungrateful, shameless wanton that she is!"

Miranda cried a protest. "Oh, no, not shameless, not wanton. She writes as if last night was the first time they embraced. They must have been so circumspect, and I do not think they can have met so very often. And she says that Huw's sister . . ."

"An ignorant baggage with no sense or morals, I do not doubt. A hill farmer! For my daughter! This descendant of a proud line!"

"Mr. Glendower says that Huw and his sister have received a liberal education and are very superior people."

At the mention of her cousin's name Mrs. Mowbray seemed to recollect herself. "My cousin! Oh, what trouble there is in this house today. I cannot ask him to pursue my daughter while his wife lies dead. And yet . . ."

She pressed the note to her lips, and Miranda, feeling pity, moved towards her. "No, don't touch me you . . . you serpent!"

"How dare you! How dare you call me by such a name. Whatever anger you feel towards Miss Ellen, I do not deserve that. I knew nothing of her plans."

"So you say. But how can a girl like you have any sense of honour? Oh, do not think I have not heard the rumours circulating this unhappy house. Last night's shameful episode in the garden has also reached my ears."

"You seem to know a great deal of servant's tittle-tattle," said Miranda, too coldly angry to guard her tongue.

Mrs. Mowbray flushed an ugly red. "Miss Bailey let it slip out, quite by chance, in my presence."

"How fortuitous of her."

"It is not your place to criticise me, Miss Miranda Courtney. And we shall see how your fine indignation crumbles when we have the doctor's report. There is more in this death than meets the eye."

There it was again—the suggestion that Lora's death could in some way be linked to her. She remembered Gethin's wild assertions that he would not let her go. That he would find a way to keep her. Surely he had not . . . could not . . . Her agonising doubt was written clearly on her expressive face, and Mrs. Mowbray gave a triumphant snort. "Yes, we shall see what we shall see. The doctor has been sent for and should soon arrive."

Miranda returned to her room to neaten her appearance before going in search of Angharad. She was surprised to find her in the schoolroom, standing at the window, staring out over the estuary. Her eyes held a curious, excited gleam as she said, "Have you heard? My mama passed away in the night. The doctor has been sent for. I wonder what he will say. Mr. Glendower is free at last, Miranda."

Miranda was shocked at what seemed the girl's unnatural calm. "Angharad, do not try to hide your distress. It is better by far to yield to emotion at a time like this."

"Emotion! I don't know what you mean. Mama was very ill, wasn't she—expected to die? I *am* sorry, of course I am. And have you heard of Cousin Ellen's behaviour. How angry Cousin Augusta is." The girl's eyes sparkled with malicious joy. "She says her daughter is ruined. She is, isn't she, Miranda. She will have to marry Mr. Craddock now, for Mrs. Pritchett says that no respectable man will have her."

"Angharad! You surely have not been chattering with the servants about so private a matter."

"And if I have! I talk to you, do I not, and I have known them a good deal longer than I have you."

Miranda had to bite her lip hard as she reminded herself that the girl was less than a child in her reactions and said only, "We cannot sit about and brood. Let us see if we can form a shell picture on velvet. It will help us to occupy our thoughts."

"I have plenty to think of, thank you, Miranda. How I smiled to see Cousin Augusta's anger. Some of it was directed at you, yet I was the only one who knew that Ellen sometimes met Mr. Craddock."

"You knew!"

"To be sure I did. I followed her and she never suspected. What a stupid girl she is, to love a common farmer and want to live in the hills with him."

At that moment Myfanwy and Gwennie carried in Miranda's breakfast, which was very late, but they volunteered no information, and she would not question them. She drank some coffee, but could not eat, and Angharad helped herself to the toast and apricot preserve and chewed with relish.

In the end Miranda felt forced to comply with Angharad's demand for a walk along the shore. As if to mock the misery at Ynys Noddfa, autumn had swung back to a day which was warm enough to be summer, and a bright sun shone from a cloudless sky onto the rippling sea. The beauty of the island was breath-taking, but it seemed to Miranda only to emphasise her sense of foreboding.

Back in the house, Angharad darted away and Gwennie

greeted Miranda as she entered the schoolroom. She looked terrified as she gabbled, "Oh, miss, the doctor's been and he's said some awful things. Mrs. Glendower felt ill last night with the colic, and Miss Bailey gave her the usual does of laudanum in Spirits of Chloroform to ease the pain, and she swears she put the bottles safely away, but the laudanum bottle was found empty by Mrs. Glendower's bed, and Dr. Jenkins is questioning everyone.

"Miss Bailey has had hysterics and said she never would harm her mistress, or be so careless as to leave the bottle by the bed, and the doctor won't believe that the mistress died a natural death, for he says she wasn't really ill at all."

Miranda sat down heavily and stared at Gwennie, whose face was pallid and shining with perspiration as she said, "Oh, miss, what will you do?"

"What will I do? I don't understand. What is there for me to do?"

Gwennie bit her knuckles then said, "Downstairs they are saying bad things. Mrs. Pritchett says that last night you had Mr. Glendower in your room and that she always knew you were here for no good. She says you saw the master as a good catch and thought that Mrs. Glendower was really very ill and would be easy to get rid of without causing suspicion."

"She's vile!" Miranda leapt to her feet and shook Gwennie till her teeth chattered. "And can you repeat such . . . such filth to me?"

"But miss . . . but miss . . ."

Miranda released Gwennie abruptly at a sound from the doorway. Gethin was outside and Miranda felt sharp hurt at the pain in his face. She wondered how long he had been there unheard; how much of the conversation had reached him, but all he said was, "Doctor Jenkins would like to see you, Miranda."

The doctor awaited her in Gethin's study, and Miranda stood facing him squarely as the keen eyes raked her face.

"Did you visit Mrs. Glendower after leaving the party last night, Miss Courtney?"

Miranda shook her head. "I saw the poor lady for the

198

last time when I helped her to her room and stayed to talk to her."

"I understand from Mr. Glendower that she told you of certain incidents in her life which she found deeply distressing. You were shocked, I do not doubt, as well as interested."

Miranda lifted her chin. "I have never asked for Mrs. Glendower's confidence and, yes, I was shocked—but only at her suffering and not by her . . . her weakness. I also understood many situations here which I had previously found puzzling. I had great sympathy for Mrs. Glendower and for . . ."

Miranda stopped and the doctor finished, "and for Mr. Glendower, were you about to say, Miss Courtney?"

Miranda nodded, and Doctor Jenkins said smoothly, "Do you know the correct dosage for laudanum?"

Again she nodded. "I was used to help in the parish at home. Our doctor there taught me much about the needs of sick people."

"And your Papa was a first-rate amateur chemist, was he not, who also taught you much?"

"Yes, he was, but . . . but I do not see . . ."

"Do you know what effect even a small overdosage of laudanum would have upon a person of an unstable nervous disposition?"

"Yes," answered Miranda quietly. "I was warned that it could have a much greater effect. Our doctor almost never advised it to be given to children because of the unpredictability of their reactions."

"And Mrs. Glendower was almost child-like in her emotions at times, was she not?"

Miranda's throat constricted, and her eyes went imploringly to Gethin. Surely he could see the implication in the doctor's line of questioning: Did he not care? He was staring out of the window and said nothing, and Doctor Jenkins finished. "That is all for now, Miss Courtney. Thank you for being so frank."

Miranda stumbled blindly from the room and stood quite still in the centre of the hall. The choking feeling was still with her. She felt as if a net had descended upon her and was strangling her in its mesh. All the doctor's questions had seemed to have one purpose—that of implicating Miranda in Lora's death. But how? Surely he did not believe her capable of such infamy! And what about Gethin? Her hands went to her cheeks. He had said nothing—not even looked at her. Could he think her so vicious as to sink to hurting Lora in any way? Then a thought struck her with the force of a blow. He had declared last night that he would not allow Miranda to leave Ynys Noddfa; that somehow he would find a way to keep her here. Had his hand been the one to end Lora's life? Had he crept into her room, half roused her from her drowsy state and, befuddled as she was by drugs, persuaded her to swallow a fatal dose of laudanum? She shuddered. What was she thinking of—of course he had not—could not—commit so iniquitous an act!

But Miranda knew that she was blameless. So how had Lora died if not by natural means? She made her way slowly to the schoolroom, where Angharad was lying full length before the fire, idly picking bits out of the rug with Miranda's sharp little embroidery scissors.

"Don't do that," ordered Miranda automatically, but she did not watch to see if she was obeyed, but sat by the fire and stared into the dancing flames.

"So what did Doctor Jenkins have to say, Miranda?"

"How do you know . . .?"

"Myfanwy told me you had been sent for. It is all very sinister, isn't it, Mama passing away so suddenly when she was not ill and the doctor suspicious, too. I wonder what will happen next?"

What did happen was not to the liking of either of them. Mrs. Mowbray bustled into the room and said sharply, "Rise to your feet, Angharad!" The girl obeyed suddenly and her cousin stared at her. "I would have supposed that you, Miranda, could have made some effort to maintain the proprieties in spite of . . . of all the trouble. Surely you could at the least have put a black armband on the child until her clothes can be dyed black or others purchased."

"I will not wear black clothes!" shrieked Angharad. "Horrid black dresses. Just because you don't mind

200

looking like a crow that is no reason for wanting to make me into one!"

"Angharad!" exclaimed Miranda, and Mrs. Mowbray together and the older woman looked coldly at Miranda. "I am perfectly well able to deal with my relative. I do not require your further help. I think you have done enough harm already."

"What do you mean?" Miranda demanded. "No, do not turn your face from me. I will not be subjected to these constant insinuations that I have committed some act of folly. I have done nothing of which I need be ashamed." She stopped abruptly, remembering the kisses and the avowals of love which had passed, however, unwillingly on her side, between herself and Gethin, and Mrs. Mowbray gave a tight smile.

"Have you not, indeed? Well, you will soon have to answer to someone else. Doctor Jenkins has left, but he has refused to certify the cause of death and has said that he must make a report to the Police Sergeant at Harlech. No doubt you have made ready a great many explanations.

"Come, Angharad, I will myself brush your hair before taking you to see your mama in her final sleep."

"No!" Angharad's eyes were wide with horror. "No, I will not look at her. You cannot make me."

Miranda put out a protesting hand as Mrs. Mowbray said, "Nonsense! In the midst of life we are in death. No one is too young to recognise that truth. You will accompany me."

Ignoring Angharad's attempts at resistance and the tears which streamed down her face, Mrs. Mowbray pulled her from the room, leaving Miranda in a state of frightened misery as great as Angharad's. She sympathised with the girl, though her cousin was merely following the custom. She got up and walked swiftly to Angharad's room. Perhaps she would run here for shelter after her ordeal and Miranda could give her comfort.

But when Angharad burst into the room a little later, she scurried about like a trapped animal, evading Miranda's outstretched arms, words tumbling from her in an almost incoherent flow. "I did not know she would look like that. I spoke to her, I called her name and she didn't answer me. I wanted her to hold me tight as she always used to. I did not know I would want that so much. I want Mama, I want her, I need her. Oh, Mama, if I had known how much I would need you I would not have put . . ."

She stopped, a hand to her mouth, and her eyes darted to Miranda's face. Miranda felt cold. "You wouldn't have put what, Angharad?"

"N . . . Nothing. I don't know what I am saying. I am too upset. That wicked Cousin Augusta . . ."

In a swift movement Miranda reached Angharad and kneeling in front of her took both the small cold hands in hers. "Angharad, darling, no one is going to hurt you, I promise you. Your Papa would never allow . . ."

"He is *not* my papa—he is not and well you know it."

"All right, my dear, yes I do know."

"And you know also that he only pretends not to care for me because he loves me so much. Now that she is gone he is free, Miranda, and he did not love her, you know, well, not since he discovered what she had done, so he will have much love to spare for . . . for someone else. Do you know, Miranda, I once overheard them in the servant's hall saying that Mr. Glendower admired you a great deal, but I kicked up such a tantrum they have not dared say it since. I made them understand that you are my friend and would not do anything bad. But in any case, Miranda, although Mama and Ellen liked you, and so of course do I, you are still only a servant and not at all suitable to be admired by a gentleman, and I made that plain to them."

Miranda swallowed hard. Every word that Angharad uttered was like a slap to her. She tried again. "Angharad, what were you going to say just now? You put . . .?"

"Leave me alone! You are unkind like all the rest. You try to make me say things . . . Oh, Miranda, I didn't mean to hurt her."

Miranda held the girl's hands in a firm grip and spoke distinctly, "What have you done?"

"The day Mama was so ill. I was the one who caused her to suffer. I did not know it would hurt her so much.

202

I put a raw mushroom, which I chopped myself, into the sauce. I knew it would upset her a little, but when she groaned it was horrible . . . horrible . . ."

"Why did you do it, Angharad?"

"I don't know really. I knew she was not strong, and I wondered if being sick would make her worse." Angharad flung herself at Miranda with such force that they almost overbalanced, and Miranda held the small shaking body close to her. "I don't know what I thought. I was wicked, wasn't I, but Mama said that she was tired of life without her lover, and I think I had an idea that I would help her to attain what she wanted. But I didn't do anything to hurt Mama this time, Miranda. When I saw how ill she was before, I did not dare do anything else."

Miranda rose and stared down at Angharad, who was crouched in a pathetic heap at her feet. To whom could she turn for help? There seemed no one now that Ellen had fled.

A commotion outside in the corridor took her to the door. Mrs. Mowbray was standing in the doorway of Lora's room, her arms spread wide as Bailey and a footman were trying to restrain someone who struggled frantically and shrieked in Welsh. Miranda realised suddenly that the scarecrow figure was Mrs. Powys, and Angharad peered past her and said, "It's Nanny! She's telling them that she helped bring her baby Lora into the world, and she is going to prepare her to leave it. Look at Cousin Augusta's face. She's disgusted!"

Miranda looked down at Angharad, who was giving a small secret smile and marvelled at the fluctuating moods of the girl. Mrs. Mowbray was answering Mrs. Powys in English, which was being translated by the footman. "Mrs. Powys, all that is necessary has been done for Mrs. Glendower. And the doctor says that she must lie in peace until . . . certain enquiries have been made."

Translated, this brought another flood of Welsh from Nanny Powys, and as Angharad listened her face became a mask of disbelief, which turned to fury as she stared up at Miranda.

"You!" she breathed. "She is saying that you . . . and my . . . Mr. Glendower—that there are rumours of you and him and that between you, you have pushed her darling Lora into eternity. You!" she repeated, backing into her room. "No, don't come near me—don't touch me. I trusted you. But you have been wicked, you and *him*—and Nanny Powys says that everyone at Ynys Noddfa knew of it. Which one of you gave my Mama the laudanum? Or did you do it together?"

On the last words her voice reached a scream, and the noise at Lora's door ceased as everyone turned in astonishment. Miranda, feeling that she could bear no more, was about to go, when Gethin arrived. He was greeted by a babel of voices, and as Miranda watched, Mrs. Mowbray and the footman left, and Bailey opened the door and closed it behind herself and Mrs. Powys.

As Gethin walked away, Miranda watched his retreating back. Her thoughts were in turmoil. He cannot believe that I killed his wife! Yet I have found myself wondering about him. And who else is there who would have a motive? For the past moments had made one thing, at least, apparent to her, that Angharad had been speaking the simple truth, and whoever had administered the fatal dose to Lora it had certainly not been she.

Chapter Fourteen

Miranda sat in Gethin's study opposite the Harlech Sergeant of Police. He was a tall man whose figure proclaimed his enjoyment of food, and at first Miranda had thought his round, high-coloured face appeared more that of a farm worker than a policeman, until she had looked into the searching eyes.

Gethin had introduced them then left them alone together. "You don't have to go, sir," Sergeant Allen had said. "Like I explained, this isn't exactly official. Doctor Jenkins simply told me he was not satisfied about the way your good lady had passed on and that he would leave the matter in my hands."

But Gethin shook his head, not meeting Miranda's eyes. "I feel it only fair to Miss Courtney that she should be free to say what she wills. She may be inhibited by my presence."

As Miranda watched him leave, she felt her heart constricted by the need for one word of kindness from him, and she turned with a deep sigh towards the policeman who was watching her closely.

He had been questioning her for some minutes, and now he continued, "So you don't think Miss Angharad had anything to do with her mother's death, Miss Courtney?"

"I have already said I do not. I told you of her words and manner."

"You are fond of the girl?"

"Yes."

"So, naturally, you would want to protect her."

"You are twisting my meaning! I do not think I could

be capable of lying to you about such an occurrence even to shield Miss Angharad, but she needs no such lies, I swear."

"Yet there was the matter of the mushrooms, Miss Courtney."

"I know, and I have told you all about that and how distressed she was when she realised what she had done. I think she would have told me everything when she broke down—if there had been more to tell."

The Sergeant looked down at his notes, and Miranda tried to bring order to her whirling thoughts. Would Angharad have kept up a deception? She had known of Huw and Ellen and had said nothing. Yet that matter did not affect her so deeply, and Miranda felt sure she was innocent this time of any wrong-doing.

"That narrows down the field somewhat then."

"I beg your pardon?"

"If Miss Angharad did not administer the laudanum to her mother, it leaves only a very few who had motive and opportunity."

"Yes." Her voice was no more than a whisper. Again a pit of horror seemed to be opening at her feet.

"From gossip I heard in the village I gathered that Miss Ellen had an eye to Mr. Glendower, should his good lady pass away, of course, which now she has done, but now I'm told she's eloped with Huw Craddock. A good man is Huw. He'll make a wife happy, I shouldn't wonder," he added reflectively.

Miranda stared at him. He was smiling at her in a kindly, yet watchful way, and she felt he was playing with her. She had once seen boys tormenting a stray dog by tying a string to its leg, allowing it to believe it had escape, then jerking it back. Was that how this man worked? She would be led into indiscretions, allowed to go so far, then tweaked back to another of his terrifying questions. Yet why should she fear? She had done no evil, she knew that. She realised that moments had passed without a word, but the Sergeant had not once taken his eyes from her face.

"You have an expressive face, Miss Courtney, just like my dear wife. Did you know I was English? I married

206

a Welsh and have spoken her lingo for years so there's no chance I might construe anything you say by my inaccurate knowledge of our mutual tongue."

"I am glad," said Miranda. Her mouth felt dry and she licked her lips.

"I hope I'm not making you nervous. This is only a chat, as you might say. Just to get the picture in my mind. After all, we can't have ladies dying without good cause, can we, even if Mrs. Glendower was so desperately ill."

"She was not! That is to say, I understood that she was physically unimpaired, though not . . . not robust."

"So she could have lived on happily for years."

"I . . . I don't know. I suppose she could, but she was not happy. The mind can have a great effect upon the body, I think. People can die of a broken heart."

There it was! The tug of the string and she had spoken without thought.

"And had the poor lady a broken heart, miss?"

"Why do you ask me? It is her husband you should be questioning about Mrs. Glendower's intimate emotions!"

"Oh, I intend to, never fear." The Sergeant snapped the last words, and his eyes fixed hers with a relentless stare.

"My wife was born in Harlech and has many relatives round about. They've told us some strange stories of a man and wife who didn't share, shall we say, connubial bliss? Stories of a very pretty young seamstress who suddenly was not merely a seamstress, but elevated to become almost a member of the family, you might say. Stories, Miss Courtney, which told of unusual doings between a master and his maid-servant."

Miranda looked speechlessly at him. Nothing she had done at Ynys Noddfa had been wilfully immoral or planned in any way, yet now she saw that, viewed from the outside, her conduct could have appeared in a very poor light.

"You are of a good family, I understand?"

"That is true."

"Isn't it odd that a girl of high birth should have come all the way to this little corner of Wales to be a servant?"

"My brother tried to . . . to force me into a marriage I found distasteful."

"Oh, you are choosy, then! Did you find Mr. Glendower's attentions distasteful?"

Miranda stood with such force that her chair tipped back and crashed to the floor. "You have no right to speak so to me! I will not endure it!"

"Sit down, please, Miss Courtney." Carefully the Sergeant put his notebook and pencil on the library table and came to pick up her chair, and Miranda sank back into it, her heart pounding in her throat.

"Of course, you don't have to stay. I can't make you. Not yet, that is. But if I don't get co-operation at Ynys Noddfa then I'm afraid I will have to make a report which could be—embarrassing—for many. See, it's like this: I've lived here a good few years now, and we all respect Mr. Glendower. So, naturally, if this business of his wife's untimely decease could be explained satisfactory, then I should be as glad as you and everyone else."

Miranda said shakily, "You say there has been—talk —in the village. If that is true, how is it that everyone still, as you say, respects my employer?"

"Well, miss, you know the way of the world. Somehow—and I'm not saying it's fair, mind you—the woman gets the blame. Mrs. Glendower has been ill a long time, but there's not been a breath of scandal until, well, to put it bluntly, miss, until you came on the scene. So we know he's a godly man not easily led into wickedness, but we don't know much about you."

Again the Sergeant consulted his notebook. "Now to go back a way, you mentioned that Mrs. Glendower wasn't a happy lady. Could you tell me a bit about that?"

"No, I could not! She made certain confidences in me the night before she died, and I will never tell you what she said. Never!"

"Never's a long time, miss. Well, I won't press you now, but in your opinion, were the confidences such as to make her take her own life?"

Miranda gasped. "I . . . I don't know. How could one possibly tell such a thing? She had endured much for

208

years. Why should she suddenly end her existence now?"

"Why indeed, Miss Courtney?"

"For God's sake, Sergeant Allen, don't torment me! If you believe I have done something wrong, then please say so and allow me to defend myself."

The Sergeant raised his brows, and his round face looked almost cherubic as he smiled. "Now I never said you'd done anything wrong, did I? You don't think that Mrs. Glendower took her own life and no more do I. I'll tell you why. When people decide to leave this vale of tears, voluntary, as you might say, they think they've good reasons. And they want the ones they leave to know what those reasons are. When I was a young policeman in London, I was called in on many of these unfortunate cases and there was nearly always a note. Sometimes, when there wasn't, it transpired that the victim, and I've always thought of such poor wretches as victims, could not read or write, but there's always been someone to say that the victim had talked of ending it all and mostly you could see for yourself that some of them had nothing to live for, poor souls. But I wouldn't have said that about the late Mrs. Glendower. She had a beautiful home, a daughter she worshipped and a kind, rich husband. What more could a lady want?"

Miranda stared at the carpet feeling weak and shaken. "I do not know," she breathed. "I do not know what more she could want. I cannot answer your questions, Sergeant Allen."

"No, I can see you're upset." His voice was kind, but she shrank from it. "I shall be talking to others of course, but the doctor isn't satisfied about Mrs. Glendower's death, and there don't seem to be many who would have found it advantageous to have her out of the way, do there?"

He snapped suddenly, "What do you think of Mrs. Mowbray?"

"What!"

"Mrs. Mowbray had an unmarriageable daughter. Perhaps she thought it might be worth her while to stage an . . . accident. Or perhaps that's what it really was. Miss Bailey might have forgotten to put the laudanum bottle away, and Mrs. G. woke up, forgot she'd had her dose, and her confusion, drunk what was left. Do you think that could have happened? I wonder if it did. I wonder who could have left the bottle so handy to her."

He spoke musingly, rubbing his chin, as if the problem were a simply hypothetical one. "You didn't answer my question, miss. The one about Mrs. Mowbray. What do you think of her?"

"She is a strong-willed lady. She is very upset about her daughter, Ellen, running off with Huw."

"You called her 'Ellen,' yet it was '*Miss* Angharad.'"

"Ellen and I were friends, but she told me nothing of her plans to elope. She is that sort of girl. She would not involve me because it would have caused me trouble."

"So you didn't know that she wasn't in the house that night?"

"No."

"And neither did her mother. H'm, that's interesting. It increases the suspects, doesn't it—if suspects is the word I want at this stage. Like I said, it's been more on the lines of a friendly chat. Thank you, Miss Courtney."

"Do you mean I can leave?"

"You can leave the room, but not the island," he said genially. "We all want this matter cleared up, don't we?"

Miranda stumbled from Gethin's study feeling drained, and almost collided with him. For a moment he held her steady and involuntarily, seeking comfort, her arms moved to encircle his neck, before he thrust her from him.

"I was coming to see why you were so long," he said smoothly. "Do you want to talk to me now, Sergeant?"

The policeman was standing in the doorway watching them. How much had he seen and what construction would he put upon it? He must move as softly as a cat, for all his size.

"Yes, I would like a word with you again, sir, if you please."

The door closed behind the two men, and Miranda turned to go. Gethin had saved her when she stumbled, as any man would have done, but she was sure he had held her unnecessarily tight and that he had been putting a severe restraint upon himself as he pushed her away.

For a second his eyes had spoken clearly of his desire before shutters of seeming indifference had veiled them.

What did he believe of her? And what did she think of him? Surely he did not consider her capable of taking Lora's life? And surely he himself could not have been so cruel. Yet how well did they really know one another?

The day dragged on. Angharad refused to talk or work with her, and Mrs. Mowbray took over her care, showing her more forebearance than Miranda would have expected. She joined the family at dinner, as usual, but could eat almost nothing. Angharad, too, had lost her appetite, and Miranda saw loathing staring at her from the girl's enormous green eyes. She would willingly have eaten alone, but Myfanwy had been sent expressly to ensure her presence. Miranda supposed that Gethin was trying to keep an appearance of normality before others.

He did not once meet her eyes, pushed the food about his plate and drank freely of the various wines, and Mrs. Mowbray spoke only when it became strictly necessary. Merrick and his unobtrusive aides brought and removed dishes with their customary deference, but Miranda avoided the stares of the servants, knowing what must be in their minds.

At last the dreadful meal was over, and she excused herself from withdrawing with the ladies and went to her room to sit by the window feeling numb with miserable apprehension, while deep within her was a canker of remorse at her inability to keep her promise to Lora to look after her child. If only she had spoken to Gethin last night and told him of her vow to Lora that she would stay at Ynys Noddfa and begged him to help her keep her honour intact, perhaps it would have prevented him from—what? There it was again! The terrible doubt that was ripping her apart. Had Gethin killed Lora for her sake? Her heart told her that he was incapable of such a malignant act, but a man in love could become mad at times. So could a woman. There were terrible newspaper stories which made this evident. And poison had always been reckoned as a woman's weapon.

Miranda discounted Mrs. Mowbray as a suspect. However much she desired a settled future for her daughter, Miranda could not see that rigid self-control breaking to the point of murder to gain her ends.

A tap came softly on her door, and she called, "Come in." Myfanwy stood before her wringing her hands.

Miranda spoke wearily. "What is it? You look ill. Has something else happened?"

"Yes! No! I don't rightly know, miss, but she was that upset. I said to Dafydd that she was more upset than seemed natural, but we decided that it was because of you, miss, you see . . ."

"No, I do not see, Myfanwy. Of whom do you speak?"

"Why, Gwennie, miss. She's been distracted by the mistress' death and earlier, when the Police Sergeant sent for her, I thought she would faint. She was that shook up when she came back, even Mrs. Pritchett was sorry for her and gave her a cordial, but now she's gone, miss."

"Gone! What do you mean? Is she out walking?"

"I don't know. All I do know is that she didn't come to servant's supper, and when I went up to our room I found her cloak gone, and I've been all round the house and can't find her, and no one's seen her for ages. Oh, miss, you don't think she . . ."

"She what?"

"Well, she thought the world of you, miss, and she told me that you had discovered the talk about . . . about you and . . . and Mr. Glendower, and she thought it would drive you away. She couldn't stand to think she'd never see you again. Oh, Miss Courtney, if only you knew how much poor Gwennie loves you, you'd understand that she'd do anything to keep you here!"

The full horror of the maid's implications twisted Miranda's stomach. "You are not suggesting . . . you cannot be insinuating that *Gwennie* did something to Mrs. Glendower!"

She sprang to her feet and began to pace the floor, scarcely hearing Myfanwy's repeated assurances of Gwennie's love for herself. Gwennie had looked more fearful than was to be expected. Had the child some idea, born of desperation, of setting her employer free to pay court to Miranda? She surely could not have gone to extreme lengths because of Miranda's simple kindness to her!

212

She cut through Myfanwy's gabble. "Could not Gwennie be somewhere on the island?"

"I think not, miss. Dafydd is the only one I've talked to, and he's been out for hours searching for her and he's been in awful trouble with Mr. Merrick for not performing his duties, but he hasn't split on Gwennie. They all think she's resting."

"Myfanwy, you are assuming altogether too much, I am sure. Now tell me, is there anywhere about the district that Gwennie could take shelter?"

"I know of only one place and that's with old Mrs. Morgan. She's been home a few times with Ceinwen, and the old lady was sorry for her and said she could come when she liked. She could be there, I daresay, for Mrs. Morgan don't care for people's talk, and she would help the poor soul."

"Help me with my cloak, Myfanwy, then ask Dafydd to guide me to the mainland. Is the tide going out? I believe it should be by now."

"You're never going to look for her, miss! It's as dark as the inside of a copper out there. Even Dafydd won't like to cross the estuary."

"Then I must go alone!" Miranda's courage almost failed her at the idea, but she was driven by the thought of Gwennie, a child whose life had been loveless until she had met her, perhaps cowering in Mrs. Morgan's cottage because she had done something terrible to help the girl she adored.

But Dafydd agreed at once to help her. He mounted his pony and led Miranda's across the estuary as the receding tide sucked greedily at the horse's hooves. More than once the ponies stumbled into shallow crevices in the sand, and once Miranda's shied, to find itself sliding at the edge of a deep pool. Dafydd was off his pony, dragging them clear, but not before Miranda tasted paralysing fear. When they arrived at Mrs. Morgan's cottage, she was helped down by Dafydd and thought for a moment that her legs would not support her. Then, drawing a deep breath, she walked towards the cottage door.

At her rap Mrs. Morgan called, "Who knocks at this ungodly hour?"

"It is I, Mrs. Morgan, Miranda Courtney. Do please let me in."

The door opened and the old woman peered out, her dark eyes gleaming in the light from the lamp she held high. "I had a notion it might be you," she said. "Who's that behind you? Dafydd is it? Good man, you'll not mind waiting outside a while. I'll give you a nip of something to warm you later."

She closed the door behind herself, and Miranda and and gestured towards the wall bed, where Gwennie lay asleep, traces of tears making small snail tracks down her cheeks.

"We can speak. She'll not wake after the brew I've given her. The poor little love is mad with fear at what she's done."

Miranda sat down heavily. "Can it be true, then, what Myfanwy seemed to fear? That Gwennie has actually done away with Mrs. Glendower?"

Mrs. Morgan gave a sharp bark of laughter. "That one! She wouldn't have the belly to put down a puppy. As it is, it has almost destroyed her to do what she has done. And now she's terrified because she's none too certain that she hasn't made matters worse for you."

Miranda was about to speak when Mrs. Morgan lifted her hand. "Wait! I thought I heard something!"

The ponies were moving restlessly, and there was the murmur of a man's voice. "It's only Dafydd," said Miranda, and Mrs. Morgan nodded.

She turned then and went to the dresser where she opened a large Bible from which she took an envelope made from thick linen paper. She handed it to Miranda. "There's a letter inside, but I can't read the English. You tell me what it says. Gwennie brought it here."

"But it cannot be for us. We have no right. Who wrote it?"

Mrs. Morgan made an explosive sound. "The plight of that pitiful creature in the bed gives us any rights, miss. If she can drive herself to the edge of madness to help you then surely you owe it to her to be equally strong. As to who wrote it—that will become clear when you read."

214

Miranda looked hesitantly from Mrs. Morgan's stern countenance to the sleeping child, then slowly drew forth the letter and began to read. She could never afterwards remember exactly what the letter said. It was written to Gethin and was from Lora. It made one thing absolutely plain—that Lora had taken her own life because she could no longer face living with the knowledge of her lover's death. She begged forgiveness from Gethin and hoped that he would find happiness in the future. Then Miranda's heart leapt at the sight of her own name, but it was mentioned only in connection with Angharad. "Please beg Miranda to remember her promise to care for my little daughter," she read, and felt sick in the knowledge of her failure.

She replaced the letter with shaking hands, feeling that she had been prying, yet unable to stem a surge of relief that the one who had been responsible for Lora's death had been herself. Suddenly she recalled the purpose of her visit. "What had this to do with Gwennie?"

"The silly little maid was with Miss Bailey when Mrs. Glendower was discovered. And during the following commotion Gwennie saw the letter. She says there has been evil talk concerning you and her master, and, indeed, I have heard it myself, and she feared for what the letter would say so she looked in it."

"But she cannot read!"

"I know that and I can't think what possessed her. The letter is in English, too, as you see, and so even her few words of Welsh had no usefulness, but it seems she recognised your name. She wept so hard I couldn't make it all out, but it had something to do with a sampler. She used to creep into your room and take it from the drawer and try to copy your name off it. You taught her where it was, she said. So that was the only word she knew. She was afeard that Mrs. Glendower had written something bad about you, so she hid the letter in her apron pocket, then when the doctor wouldn't agree the death was natural, and the Police Sergeant came, Gwennie was horrified at what she'd done and didn't know how to undo any harm. She still didn't know what the letter said so she came here to ask Ceinwen, not knowing that my granddaughter is visiting relatives tonight. She nearly got caught by the incoming tide, too—that girl loves you, miss, so I hope you'll not be hard on her."

Miranda sat quite still for several moments allowing a full flood of relief to wash over her. Later she would allow her pity for Lora to take its place, but now she could only rejoice that the suspicion and questions were over.

"We must give the letter to Mr. Glendower as soon as possible, and he will see that Sergeant Allen reads it," she murmured.

There was a sharp rap on the door, and Mrs. Morgan went grumbling to answer. "I told you, Dafydd, to bide out there. I was just going to get you a brew." She opened the door as she spoke, and her voice trailed away. "You! I suppose you've been listening. Nasty, prying sort of job you've got!"

"But a very necessary one, Mrs. Morgan," said Sergeant Allen as he stepped over the threshold. "I'll take that letter, Miss Courtney."

She handed it to him. "How did you find me?"

"Oh, I never lost you, in a manner of speaking. I was waiting on the mainland to see who ran first from Ynys Noddfa. I sent a man after Gwennie to follow where she went, then we waited to see who would be next. And here I am. And I've heard what was said. And now, if you'll excuse me for a minute, I'll read the letter for myself."

He shook his head, tutting gently. "Poor lady; poor, poor lady. I wondered if she had done away with herself, but, if you remember, it was the absence of this very letter that puzzled me. Gwennie has been a very naughty girl. A lot of trouble she's caused me. She should leave such things to her superiors."

"She won't get into trouble, will she? She meant no harm."

Sergeant Allen smiled. "I'll make it easy for her, miss. I've a girl of my own Gwennie's age, and her life's been easy compared with that little waif's."

He looked at her so benignly that Miranda said quaveringly, "Did . . . did you ever suspect me of so evil an act as . . ."

"Murder? Well, not really, miss. I gave you more than one escape route, but you didn't act like a guilty party seeking a way out. You were insistent that Miss Angharad was innocent and wouldn't believe Mrs. Mowbray could be so ruthless. And even when I suggested suicide you didn't leap on the idea as a road out of your troubles. So, I thought to myself, her actions aren't those of a guilt-laden soul. But I had my duty to do, miss, and that silly chit"—nodding towards the sleeping Gwennie—"didn't help any."

He and Dafydd gulped down the hot posset prepared by Mrs. Morgan, and Miranda gratefully drank a cup of tea before allowing Dafydd to lead her pony back across the estuary. The tide was almost right out and the sand drying in the night wind. Sergeant Allen went to tell Gethin of the latest turn of events, and Miranda went straight to her room, feeling too exhausted to do anything more than undress and fall into her soft bed.

She slept, but awoke feeling unrefreshed and torn by conflicting emotions. Pity for Lora; apprehension for Angharad, who so badly needed love and understanding and whom circumstances had caused to hate Miranda; and for Gethin—love which did not waver. Even when she was tortured by the terror that his agony of mind had driven him to a desperate, despicable act, she could not stifle her love for him. But now there was a barrier between them which seemed insurmountable, born as it was of the intangibles of despair and mistrust.

She scarcely knew what to do so followed her routine of going to the schoolroom. It was empty and she simply sat in front of the fire, idly staring into the flames, until approaching footsteps made her turn to see Mrs. Mowbray ushering a protesting Angharad into her room.

Mrs. Mowbray looked ill, and Miranda rose instinctively to her feet to allow the older woman to take her place, but Mrs. Mowbray remained standing. "I am not one to mince words, Miranda. I heard last night that my poor, misguided cousin took her own life."

Miranda gestured towards Angharad, who was fixing her with a sullen gaze, but Mrs. Mowbray continued, "This child already knows far more than she should. It was thought wisest to tell the truth of her mother's demise so that no misunderstanding should linger in her brain. Such as it is," she added in an undertone.

"She has been informed with certainty that you and her . . . Mr. Glendower were in no way responsible for the terrible tragedy which has overtaken this house." She looked round as Myfanwy entered. "Ah, there you are. Please take Miss Angharad walking and see that she is warmly clad. Fresh air will do her more good than moping around indoors."

Angharad trailed out with unusual docility, and alone, the two women regarded each other. Mrs. Mowbray spoke first. "I cannot pretend to like you, Miranda, though I admit that my feelings may be unjust. Time will tell, perhaps. You probably look upon me as a hard woman." She sat down now and was silent for a while. "Events have made me hard, Miranda. To imagine oneself the wife of a successful man, then to awake one morning, a widow without means of support and a daughter to marry off who is only moderately passable in appearance is a bitter experience for a woman. I said I have not liked you, but I can and do respect you for the way you have fought your own adverse circumstances."

Again she was silent for a moment. "Well, that is not what I came to say. I have been awake half the night thinking and decided that my best course would be to offer to care for Angharad. Mr. Glendower agrees with me—at least until this foolish passion the child has for him has passed. Maybe she can one day return to Ynys Noddfa. Again, time will tell."

Miranda murmured something incoherent, but Mrs. Mowbray was quick to catch her thought. "You fear that I will not give Angharad the loving kindness she needs. You are wrong. I have explained why I have been so hard, but now there will no longer be any need, Mr. Glendower has said that he will make me a generous allowance for life. Ellen will be married . . ." Her voice broke and Miranda stepped towards her. "I love—loved —my daughter, Miranda, though you may find that difficult to believe. I will give Angharad, with her poor undeveloped mind, the devotion I would offer any helpless

218

child. And I will try to rekindle her love for you." She shot Miranda a piercing look. "It may be necessary for her to care for you, may it not?"

Miranda did not falter. "I cannot tell you, Mrs. Mowbray. So much has happened—I am confused—I see nothing clearly."

Mrs. Mowbray kept her eyes on Miranda's face as she nodded twice. "You are not the girl I imagined, I think. It seems that, after all, you do not grab at the riches which surely must lie within your reach."

She stared into the flames, sighed and said, "It seems we must all wait upon the future."

Spring had come to Wales, and Miranda sat on an outcrop of sun-warmed rock, high in the mountains, staring down into the valley. After Lora's death she had gratefully accepted an invitation from Ellen and Huw to stay with them for as long as she wished, and the grey stone farmhouse had not only given her shelter from the winter storms, but had established a tranquility which she needed to assemble her scattered thoughts and see the past in perspective. Ellen was glad of her company and the help she offered in a home where servants were not numerous. Ellen was expecting Huw's child, and the news had brought from her mother a letter which had given peaceful ease to her face.

Perhaps because of the shocks she had received, Angharad's brain had ceased to develop; in fact, there had appeared to be some reversion, and she was no longer so precocious. She and her elderly cousin seemed to have found unexpected rapport.

Gwennie was forgiven her wrongs and had accompanied Miranda to the farm, where she was fast blossoming into a comely girl turning the heads of several young shepherds.

Ceinwen had taken advantage of a short spell of mild weather soon after Christmas to ride up with the news of Nanny Powys's death. "Poor old body," she said, as she sat eating in the farmhouse kitchen, "she was glad to go, they say. She wanted to follow her beloved Miss Lora. She asked to look after Miss Angharad, but they refused to allow it. They were right, I know, but she sickened and died soon after. Mr. Glendower tried to send her necessities in her last days, but she'd have none of them. She died still hating him—and he not deserving of it."

She finished a bite of cheese before she went on. "I didn't come only to tell you of death, though. After Nanny Powys was put in the churchyard, my granny called for some of the village women to come and talk to her and without wagging her tongue too much made them realise that poor Mrs. Glendower's dreadful action had nothing to do with you. Well, there've been rumours enough of the past, long before you came, and they respect my old granny, so they do."

Miranda felt moved. "How good of her to think of me so kindly," she exclaimed. "How is she, Ceinwen?"

"She'll not stir out of doors till Spring," Ceinwen had grinned, "but though her body may be weak, there's nothing wrong with her brain. She was careful to choose the women who talk loudest and hold most sway round here, so, never fear, Miss Courtney, that when you choose to come down from the mountain, anyone will point an evil finger at you."

"How . . . how is Mr. Glendower?" Miranda dared to ask, and Ceinwen directed her a shrewd glance.

"He's in mourning as a good widower should be. He's well respected for showing deference for his dead since it was pretty well known that he and his wife had not lived ideally together. I think that if . . . if he should decide to look about him for another—companion—for his future, it would be taken as quite natural."

She did not wait for a response, but wiping her mouth with her handkerchief, went to the parlour to thank Ellen for her hospitality. Then she swung herself to the back of her pony and began the ride home.

Now Miranda sat thinking of the past as she so often did. She had not seen Ynys Noddfa for six months nor heard from its master. They had parted in pain. Gethin had held her hands and kissed her gently on her white cheek, before finding her lips. She had scarcely responded. The barrier which had been fashioned by evil tongues and their own harrowing doubts could not easily be torn down.

He had sent Mrs. Pritchett and Merrick away, setting them up in a business in South Wales, where they had married. Miranda felt great doubt as to their felicity, but that was not her worry, and she still felt shudders run through her body as she remembered their spite towards her.

Gethin had spoken briefly before Dafydd led her pony from the island. "We are too close to the cruel events of the past days to talk of our feeling for one another. It must have seemed to you that I held you in suspicion. I could never think you capable of wickedness, my dear, but we were both confused and I dared not approach you, even to speak as I wished, with so many eyes upon us. I am convinced as I am of my life, that I love you, Miranda, but I will not press you for answers now. In any case it would not be seemly. I owe poor Lora the respect of mourning her, though I will not pretend, to you, feelings of grief that do not exist. Yet, believe me, when I say, Miranda, that caring for you, helped me for the first time, fully to understand her despair over Ifan. Before you came to me, I was not always gentle with Lora and have episodes in my memory which shame me now."

Miranda had stood looking up into his lined face, unable to find words to express the hopes and longings which splintered her heart; unable to give voice to her faith that somewhere in the tangle of her emotions there was a steadfast love for him.

Before they parted, Gethin said, "Be happy with Ellen, my dear. We will give ourselves until the Spring to decide, then surely we shall have the answer to our future.

"I know what I feel for you, but if by some chance, some unimaginable chance, I lose my faith in the possibility of our finding joy together, I will not distress you by my presence, but will send a message. Will you do the same for me?"

She had nodded, tears filling her eyes, and he lifted her hand to his lips, before allowing her to cross the estuary sands for what might be the last time.

And now Spring was here. It was in the blossoming hill flowers, in the snow-swelled streams hurrying to the sea, in the lambs which amused her with their antics. Suddenly the bleakness of winter had yielded before the sun, and for three days she had come here to sit and stare down the valley through which a messenger must come to her.

At first she mistrusted her eyes in the brightness of the sun, but she stood swiftly as she saw a solitary horseman approaching. Of course men came to the farm; men carrying letters, provisions, but surely the mount she could see in the distance was larger than the customary sturdy Welsh pony. Her heart began to thud against her ribs as she shielded her eyes and tried to penetrate the space between them with an unwavering stare.

The horseman came closer and now there were no more doubts. Gethin was riding up the hill towards her, and since he himself had chosen to come, it could mean only one thing. That he loved her as deeply as she now knew she loved him, and that nothing that had gone before, or would happen in the future, could diminish that love.

She gave a cry of joy, heard only by the sheep, stretched out her arms in a gesture of welcome, before holding her skirts clear of the bracken, she began to run down the hill to meet her destiny.

Dorothy Eden

Ms. Eden's novels have enthralled millions of readers for many years. Here is your chance to order any or all of her bestselling titles direct by mail.

☐ AN AFTERNOON WALK	23072-4	1.75
☐ DARKWATER	23153-4	1.75
☐ THE HOUSE ON HAY HILL	X2839	1.75
☐ LADY OF MALLOW	Q2796	1.50
☐ THE MARRIAGE CHEST	23032-5	1.50
☐ MELBURY SQUARE	22973-4	1.75
☐ THE MILLIONAIRE'S DAUGHTER	23186-0	1.95
☐ NEVER CALL IT LOVING	23143-7	1.95
☐ RAVENSCROFT	22998-X	1.50
☐ THE SHADOW WIFE	22802-9	1.50
☐ SIEGE IN THE SUN	Q2736	1.50
☐ SLEEP IN THE WOODS	23075-9	1.75
☐ SPEAK TO ME OF LOVE	X2735	1.75
☐ THE TIME OF THE DRAGON	23059-7	1.95
☐ THE VINES OF YARRABEE	23184-4	1.95
☐ WAITING FOR WILLA	23187-9	1.50
☐ WINTERWOOD	23185-2	1.75

Buy them at your local bookstores or use this handy coupon for ordering:

FAWCETT PUBLICATIONS, P.O. Box 1014, Greenwich Conn. 06830

Please send me the books I have checked above. Orders for less than 5 books must include 60c for the first book and 25c for each additional book to cover mailing and handling. Orders of 5 or more books postage is Free. I enclose $_____ in check or money order.

Mr/Mrs/Miss_____

Address_____

City_____ State/Zip_____

Please allow 4 to 5 weeks for delivery. This offer expires 6/78.

A-5